The Lady of Fire
and Tears

D0109599

Terry Deary was born in Sunderland and now lives in County Durham, where the Marsdens of *Tudor Terror* lived. Once an actor, he has also been a teacher of English and drama and has led hundreds of drama workshops for children in schools. He is the author of the phenomenally bestselling *Horrible Histories* and of many other successful books for children, both fiction and non-fiction.

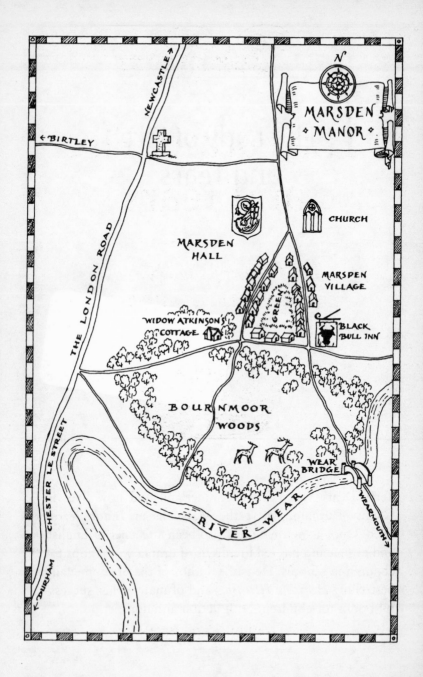

The Lady of Fire and Tears

Terry Deary

Illustrated by Hemesh Alles

Orion Children's Books
and

Dolphin Paperbacks

First published in Great Britain in 1998
as an Orion hardback
and a Dolphin paperback
by Orion Children's Books
a division of the Orion Publishing Group Ltd
Orion House
5 Upper St Martin's Lane
London WC2H 9EA

Second impression 1998

A catalogue record for this book is available
from the British Library

Printed in Great Britain by
Clays Ltd, St Ives plc

Contents

All chapter titles are quotations from *King Henry VI*, Part 2. This play was written by William Shakespeare for Queen Elizabeth I of England, about five years after the execution of Mary Queen of Scots. It is a warning about the dangers of plotting against a rightful monarch. Will Shakespeare knew how to please his queen!

The Marsden Family vii

CHAPTER ONE 1
"Barren winter, with his wrathful nipping cold"

CHAPTER TWO 9
"Foul felonious thief that fleeced poor passengers"

CHAPTER THREE 18
"Like any devil, he will spare neither man, woman, nor child"

CHAPTER FOUR 27
"I should rejoice now at this happy news!"

CHAPTER FIVE 36
"And torture him with grievous lingering death"

CHAPTER SIX 45
"Desperate thieves, all hopeless of their lives"

CHAPTER SEVEN 57
"And roughly send to prison the immediate heir of England"

CHAPTER EIGHT 69
"The treasure of thy heart"

CHAPTER NINE 78
"O barbarous and bloody spectacle!"

CHAPTER TEN 89
"Be poisonous too and kill thy forlorn queen"

CHAPTER ELEVEN 100
"I hope you'll come to supper"

CHAPTER TWELVE 110
"Here's a pot of good double beer"

CHAPTER THIRTEEN 119
"Cut out his tongue for cogging"

CHAPTER FOURTEEN 131
"Away, you cutpurse rascal, you filthy bung, away!"

CHAPTER FIFTEEN 142
*"Till the axe of death hang over thee,
as sure it shortly will"*

CHAPTER SIXTEEN 155
"O, torture me no more I will confess"

CHAPTER SEVENTEEN 167
"And here pronounce free pardon to them all"

CHAPTER EIGHTEEN 176
"This my death may never be forgot"

The Historical Characters 187

The Time Trail 190

The Marsden Family

WILLIAM MARSDEN *The narrator*
The youngest member of the family. Training to be a knight as his ancestors were before him, although the great days of knighthood are long gone. His father insists on it and Great-Uncle George hopes for it. But he'd rather be an actor like the travelling players he has seen in the city. He can dream.

Grandmother **LADY ELEANOR MARSDEN**
She was a lady-in-waiting to Queen Anne Boleyn. After seeing the fate of her mistress she came to hate all men, she married one, maybe out of revenge. Behind her sharp tongue there is a sharper brain. She is wiser than she looks.

Grandfather **SIR CLIFFORD MARSDEN**
He was a soldier in Henry VIII's army where (Grandmother says) the batterings softened his brain. Sir Clifford is the head of the family although he does not manage the estate these days he simply looks after the money it makes. He is well known for throwing his gold around like an armless man.

Great-Uncle **SIR GEORGE SULGRAVE**
A knight who lost his lands and now lives with his stepsister, Grandmother Marsden. He lives in the past and enjoys fifty-year-old stories as much as he enjoys fifty-year-old wine. He never lets the truth stand in the way of a good story.

SIR JAMES MARSDEN *William's father*
He runs the Marsden estate and is magistrate for the district. He believes that, without him, the forces of evil would take over the whole of the land. This makes him a harsh and humourless judge. As a result he is as popular as the plague.

LADY MARSDEN *William's mother*
She was a lady-in-waiting to Mary Queen of Scots. Then she married Sir James. No one quite knows why. She is beautiful, intelligent, caring and witty. Quite the opposite of her husband and everyone else in the house.

MARGARET "MEG" LUMLEY
Not a member of the family, but needs to be included for she seems to be involved in all the family tales. A poor peasant and serving girl, but bright, fearless and honest (she says). Also beautiful under her weather-stained skin and the most loyal friend any family could wish for (she says).

The Lady of Fire and Tears

CHAPTER ONE

"Barren winter, with his wrathful nipping cold"

When winter came to Marsden Hall we would huddle round the fire and tell tales. The fire roared in the huge stone hearth of the main hall and lit the faces of the family. The draught from the windows and the doors made the tapestries on the walls ripple. The bright embroidered figures seemed to come alive then and walk across the fields of green silk. They were ghosts that had come to listen to our stories.

The Marsden family stories were not like the stories your family tell. Our stories were true. The laughter and the tears, the mysteries and the fears, were real. When I was a boy I listened to those stories and they haunted my dreams. Even now, years later, as I write them down I can see the family gathered there in the flickering amber light. I can feel the warmth of the fire on my face and the cold of the winter air on my back. And I can feel the chill of fear that ran down my spine as I listened to some of those sad stories.

I can see the flowing white beard of Great-Uncle George as he roared out his tales of ancient battles the Marsden family had fought through the years. I can hear Grandmother's creaking voice chilling us with her memories of the muderous Henry VIII. Grandfather thrilled us with stories of his adventures in the lawless wilderness that was the border with Scotland. Father boasted about his travels and bored us with his battles against the miserable criminals who lived their secret lives in our part of Durham County in the north east of England. He was the magistrate who brought them to justice – when he could catch them.

"They respect me," he said.

"They hate him," our orphaned serving girl, Meg, used to say.

But most of all I remember my mother's stories. She was the quietest of the storytellers, yet some of her stories were so terrifying that they froze my blood.

"Tell me about Mary Queen of Scots," I would beg her.

"I've told it a dozen times or more, William," she would say with a sad smile.

"I haven't heard it," Meg said one winter night at the turn of the century when old Queen Elizabeth was dying.

My mother frowned. I knew she hated the story. And I knew she had to tell it, over and over again. When we are sick the doctors open a vein and let out the blood to let out the disease. In telling her story I think Mother wanted to let out the pain that was in her heart.

I had heard the story before, it was true, and I'd repeated it to Meg one evening when we were playing backgammon in my room. But Meg wanted to hear it from my mother herself. "Tell me," she said.

Mother folded her embroidery, placed it in her lap, and folded her hands over it. I lowered my eyes because I couldn't bear to see the hurt in her face. But Meg turned her great sea-green eyes up to look at my mother, pushed her tangled mane of chestnut hair back from her forehead and rested her pointed chin on one hand.

"I was there when they executed Mary Queen of Scots," my mother began. "It was just before I married your father, Will, and before you were born, of course. It was at this time of the year, February. Fifteen eighty-seven, the year before the Great Armada tried to conquer us.

I was with Queen Mary in her room when the Earl of
Shrewsbury came to her that night – a bitter, mid-winter
night like tonight – and told her she would die at dawn,
at eight o'clock."

"Where was this?" Meg asked.

"Fortheringhay Castle in Northamptonshire, two hundred miles south of here. A bleak enough place at the best
of times, but when you're a prisoner waiting for your execution it is a cold Hell."

"So she knew she was going to die," Meg said.

"Queen Elizabeth had imprisoned her for eighteen years,
always threatening to execute her and never having the
courage to sign the order. Queen Mary thought she would
die a natural death in her prison. She'd already retired to
bed that February night. She suffered terribly from rheumatism and needed all my help to rise and get dressed to meet
the earl. When he came into her apartment he had the
warrant with the yellow wax seal of England on it."

"I couldn't stand that," Meg whispered. "Knowing
that you're going to be executed in a few hours' time. It's
horrible."

"Queen Mary took the news calmly enough," said my
mother. "She asked for a Catholic priest so she could say

◆ 3 ◆

her final prayers. They refused to allow it, of course."

I shook my head. "It couldn't have done any harm. Not then."

"Queen Elizabeth was spiteful. Queen Mary asked to be buried in France, but even that was refused. All she was given were those twelve hours to prepare herself. I wrote down her requests – she divided up her clothes among her friends and servants. I still have the dress she gave me, Will. It's in a chest in my room. I've never worn it and I can't bear to look at it, but if you find it one day then you'll know it belonged to a sad lady."

"Did she deserve to die?" Meg asked.

My mother took a deep breath. "We all dressed in black and spent the night with her. We took it in turns to read to her from her Bible. We ended with the story of Jesus dying on the cross, and the good thief who died on the cross alongside him. Then Queen Mary said a curious thing. She said, 'That thief was a great sinner – but not such a great sinner as I have been.' So, Meg, I suppose she thought she deserved to die."

"But not that way," said Meg.

"The Queen lay back on the bed and closed her eyes. She couldn't sleep, of course. Not with the marching of the guards outside her door, and the hammering of the carpenters in the great hall. She must have known they were finishing the scaffold that she'd be executed on. She rose at six o'clock and said her prayers alone. At eight she asked me to go with her to the hall. What could I say? I didn't want to see her die, but I couldn't refuse, could I?"

My mother was trembling. Meg touched her hand gently. "No, you couldn't," she murmured.

"We dressed her in her black satin dress. The buttons were black jet trimmed with pearls and made in the shape of acorns. Lovely things. And the sleeves of the dress were slashed to show the purple lining underneath. She had a white veil flowing down her back like a bride. She was a bride going to be married to death."

"Was she afraid?" Meg asked.

"She didn't seem to be. She looked so calm. She petted her little dog and walked down those cold corridors to the great hall."

"They'd have had to carry me," Meg said.

"I didn't know there would be so many people there," my mother said. "Three hundred people crowded into the great hall. The death of a queen is a moment of history. So many people, so quiet. And staring at her. Watching every last movement. Listening to that foolish man, the Dean of Peterborough."

"What did he do?"

"He preached at her and told her to give up her Catholic religion. On and on he went. She simply answered, 'I've lived a Catholic, so I will die a Catholic.'"

"That's what I'd have told him," Meg said fiercely.

"But you're not a Catholic," I reminded her.

She glared at me. "No, but if I *was* then I wouldn't give it up when some miserable Protestant was going to chop off my head, would I?"

"No, I suppose not."

"The scaffold was waist high and hung with black cloth. The Queen needed the help of a guard to climb the stairs ... it was the rheumatism, not fear, that made it so hard for her. Then I had to help take off her black dress. She was wearing a red petticoat and a red bodice. The bodice was cut low at the back so the axe ..."

My mother stopped. Her eyes were filled with tears, as they always were at this point of the story. She sniffed away the tears and went on, "She slipped on red satin sleeves and then we had to step down from the platform. Time had passed so slowly all that night, and all through the prayers and the dean's speeches. But then it seemed to speed up. It was rushing her towards her death and I could no more stop it than I could stop the river rushing by at Durham. They covered her head in a white cloth like a turban and laid it on the block. I turned away then. I couldn't watch, I couldn't."

"I know," said Meg comfortingly.

"I heard the sound of the axe. Three times it fell. I remember the silence. Then there was the tiny sound of Queen Mary's dog whimpering. It had followed her from her apartment and had been hiding beneath her skirts."

My mother pulled a handkerchief from her sleeve and dabbed at her eyes. "It was all a long time ago, Meg. She died so England could be safe for people like you and Will."

"It still upsets you to remember, though, doesen't it?" the girl asked.

My mother picked up her embroidery and began work with the needle again. "It was a horrible way to die," she said slowly. "But there are worse. No, that's not what upsets me."

"What is it?" I asked.

My mother was calm again and smiled softly. "One day I may tell you, Will."

"And me," Meg said.

"And you, Meg."

"Why not now?" I demanded.

"Because it's time I made sure supper is ready," my mother told me. "Come along, Meg, you can help me prepare the table."

"Oh, Mother!" I cried. "I hate mysteries!"

Her eyes were sparkling now. "I thought you loved them."

"I mean I hate mysteries that I don't know the answer to. Tell us now why the story upsets you after so many years."

My mother rose and placed the embroidery on the table beside her. "It upsets me, Will, because I helped kill Mary Queen of Scots."

I believe my mouth fell open and for a minute my lips refused to work. "You swung the axe!" I gasped.

"No. But I was part of the plot to have her executed. I'll always believe I could have done more to stop her being killed. And, because I didn't stop the execution, I'm as guilty as anyone of her death. I helped kill Mary Queen of Scots."

She brushed strands of embroidery silk off her dark-blue woollen dress and turned towards the passage to the kitchen. "But what did you do?" I asked.

She stopped at the door and turned. Meg was looking up at her, fascinated. "That, William, is another story for another time. I've never told anyone the full story, and I'm not sure I want to now."

◆ 7 ◆

Before I could object she turned and walked through the door. Meg looked at me, raised her dark eyebrows in an expression of helplessness, then turned to hurry after her mistress.

I think I would never have heard my mother's story if it hadn't been for something that happened to Meg a little later.

CHAPTER TWO

"Foul felonious thief that fleeced poor passengers"

My father entered the library without knocking and interrupted my Latin lesson. My tutor, Master Benton, bowed his balding head. "Sir James, what an honour," he said.

My father's thin face was sour as vinegar. "The lesson is finished, Master Benton," he snapped.

"Indeed, Sir James. And I must say that your son has a fine grasp of his irregular verbs."

My father looked through the window across the lawn that was still white with the morning frost. "That's good. He'll need Latin to study the law."

"Exactly what I keep telling him," my tutor said smoothly.

"You can go now, Master Benton."

"And he needs Latin to understand his history texts and his religious books. A skill in Latin is such a precious gift!" Master Benton went on.

"Quite. Quite. You are doing a good job, Master Benton. But if you would like to leave us now, I wish to talk to my son."

"Of course, Sir James." Master Benton turned to me. "Now, I want you to learn this page of your book before I return next week."

I nodded. Latin bored me. I had no use for it. I would not be studying the law or history or religion. I wanted to become an actor. One day I'd made the mistake of mentioning this idea to my father, and his face turned purple with rage. He told me that my duty would be to take over the management of the Marsden Manor estates when I was old enough. We had never mentioned the subject again. In fact he hardly ever spoke to me on any subject. His visit to my lesson was bound to bring unwelcome news.

As the tutor bowed and backed out of the room, my father went to the door and looked down the corridor to make sure we were alone. He turned, paced across the room, turned again and paced back. At last he stopped with his back to the small fire that scarcely warmed the library. "I am being made to look a fool," he said suddenly.

"Really?" I said, looking up from my books on the table. "That must be difficult." My father glared at me, suspecting that I was poking fun at him.

"Marsden Manor has always been one of the most peaceful places in the north of England. I am well known for keeping the peace. I am firm with criminals so honest people can go about their business without fear. I am respected by everyone."

"Except the men you have hanged," I said.

"Exactly!" he cried, as if I had praised him. "The people who do *not* respect me find themselves swinging from the gallows. That's a lesson they won't forget in a hurry."

"It's a lesson they won't forget for as long as they live," I agreed.

"I sit in judgement on about ten cases every week. Mainly beggars and brawlers and traders who try to cheat their customers. But suddenly, since the turn of the year, I have been flooded with complaints. Flooded! In the past week there have been ten houses robbed, washing stolen from bushes where it was laid out to dry, cups and coins taken from locked chests. Two farmers have been robbed of their money on their way back from Chester-le-Street market and five purses cut from belts at the market. I tell you, William, something evil has come into this region and I am going to root it out. I am going to destroy it."

"Whom do you suspect?" I asked. "One of the villains in the Black Bull Tavern?"

"I suspect *all* the villains in the Black Bull Tavern," he snarled.

"You could hang them all. Then if the crimes went on you'd know they weren't to blame," I suggested.

Only my father could be vicious enough to take my idea seriously. "I have thought about it," he said. "But a magistrate who hangs too many criminals is not popular with the other gentlemen in the country. A man must be firm but not cruel. That's the way I've always been. But Lord Birtley didn't hang a single man, woman or child last year – and he goes about *boasting* of the fact! Boasting! As if being merciful were a good thing!"

"That's what it says in the Bible, of course," I reminded him.

I felt the full heat of his glare again. "Lord Birtley didn't have this wicked rabble breaking into *his* home and stealing *his* best silver from under *his* very nose."

Suddenly I began to understand my father's rage. "We've been burgled?"

"That's what I just said, didn't I? But they have gone too far this time. No one steals from Sir James Marsden and escapes without a rope round his neck."

"What happened?" I asked.

"That's what we're going to find out."

"We?"

"I need your help," he said. My father gave orders, bullied and threatened. But he had never before asked me for help.

"What can I do?"

"I do not want to bring witnesses into a public court. I do not want everyone to know that I have been robbed. I do not want them laughing at me. I want a private hearing. I want it here in the hall at Marsden, but I want the trial to be conducted properly. I have asked Constable Smith to arrest the suspect. I want you to be my clerk and make a written record when I examine her."

"You have a suspect already?" I asked, gathering some sheets of parchment, a quill and a pot of ink. "Who?"

My father marched towards the door. "That dreadful serving girl. The orphan we rescued from the poor house. And how does she repay us? By stealing from us!"

"Meg?" I gasped. "Meg Lumley? She stole from us?"

"She was part of the plot," my father said as he strode along the corridor and down the stairs towards the hall. "You'll see, you'll see."

He pushed open the oak doors into the great hall. I walked behind him, struggling to keep my writing equipment in my hands. Meg stood facing the table that stood in the bow of the window. The huge red-faced Constable Robyn Smith was still dressed in his leather blacksmith's apron, which was stretched like a drum across his belly. His thick beard was singed and curled at the front where he leaned over the fire each day. He looked unhappy.

Meg's face showed no feelings at all. She was a little paler than usual, but her hands were folded calmly across the front of her faded black dress. For a moment her eyes flickered towards me as I sat by my father's side at the table. I thought I saw some disappointment in them, but I may have imagined it. She grew watchful again.

My father cleared his throat and waited impatiently for me to spread the parchment on the table, dip the quill in the ink and prepare to write. Before he could start, the door opened quietly and my mother slipped into the hall. "This is no place for you, Marion," my father said harshly.

"It's my home, James," she replied quietly.

"Today it's a court of law."

"And a court of law is open to the public. If I can't enter as mistress of the house, then I will be here as a member of the public."

My father's eyes bulged, but he said, "The more witnesses the better, Marion. I don't want it to be said that I hold secret trials!"

"Quite!" She smiled and sat at the hearth.

My father cleared his throat again. "Margaret Lumley, commonly known as Meg Lumley, you have been brought here today to answer a charge that you did steal a silver cup to the value of five pounds. What have you to say for yourself?"

I expected Meg to answer with a show of temper, but her quiet voice was even more frightening. "If I stole the cup, then where is it?"

"We don't have to produce the cup," my father said cleverly. "*You* do. It was last seen in your hands."

"I was cleaning it," she said.

My father turned to me. "Hah! Make sure you get that! She admits she had the cup."

"There was a tap on the window," she explained, "and it was Michael the Taverner wanting to speak to me. I went to the door to see what he wanted."

"And you handed him the cup!" my father said.

"No. I left it on the table. Michael said he wanted me to go round to the stables for a quiet word, so I followed him."

"So, why couldn't he have this quiet word at the door?"

"He was afraid you might arrive. He says you hate him and would have him thrown out."

"I would indeed," Father sneered. "This is an unlikely story, but, for the records, will you tell the court what he wanted with you?"

"He wanted to know if I needed some extra money. He said I could help serve food and ale at the Black Bull when I had finished work here."

My father's eyes narrowed. "Ah, he did, did he?"

"I said I'd ask my mistress if she minded. But when I came back to the kitchen, the cup I'd left on the table had gone!"

"And you expect us to believe that?" my father said, taunting her.

Now I saw the anger begin to rise in her sea-green eyes. She stepped forward and Robyn the Blacksmith placed a huge red hand on her shoulder. "With respect, sir, it is a common thieves' trick," he said. "Send someone to take a maid away from her work while an assistant nips into the house and steals whatever is about."

My father smiled. "Thank you, Constable Smith. It is also a common thieves' trick for a servant to hand her master's goods to an accomplice and share the money they get for it. In this case that seems more likely, I think."

Meg struggled to free herself from the constable's grip, but she was as helpless as a fly in a spider's web. "Why would I want to steal from you? I love Lady Marsden like my own mother!" she cried.

"And children have been known to steal from their parents," Father smiled. "I think you have failed to prove your innocence. I therefore sentence you to hang by the neck until you are dead."

The silence in the room was sudden and total. I stopped scratching with the quill, Meg stopped her struggle and it seemed everyone had stopped breathing.

I was the first to speak. "Father! You can't!"

"Quiet, boy!" he said. His voice was cold, hard and cutting

as a steel sword. "There is only one way in which you can save your miserable little neck," he went on, looking at the girl. She was swaying unsteadily.

"How?" she asked. Her voice was a faint croak.

"You can give information against your accomplices. Tell me that Michael the Taverner was part of this plot with you. He will hang while you will simply spend a term imprisoned at Durham."

"But I can't say that!" Meg whispered. "It isn't true!"

My father spread his hands as if he were helpless. "I cannot be any fairer than that," he said. "If you *are* telling the truth, then there is only one other thing you can do. Find me the thief."

"You'd have to set me free to do that," Meg said.

"I could let you go free for a week," Father offered. "If you haven't found the guilty man at the end of that time, then you hang. If you *do* find him, you'll get ten per cent of the value of the cup. Ten shillings, Meg! Nearly as much as you earn in a year!"

Her green eyes were flickering round the room as she thought about the offer. "How can *I* find out who stole the cup when you can't?"

My father rubbed his hands suddenly with a brisk show of delight. "You can take the job in the Black Bull Tavern. It's a nest of vipers. You will report back everything that you discover about the highway robberies, the cutpurses, the house-breakings and all the other crimes that have been committed in this district since the New Year." He stood up and snatched the parchment from the table. "I'll keep this paper for a week. It says here that you admit leaving the cup for a thief to take. That's enough to hang you. At the end of the week, you bring me the thief and I'll tear up the confession."

My father walked round the table till he stood in front of the girl. He leaned forward and grinned. "Don't try to run away, or I will have you pursued and executed on the spot. And don't fail at the Black Bull, or I'll show the whole county of Durham what happens to servants who steal from this master." He looked across at the blacksmith. "Release her, Robyn."

The blacksmith let go of Meg, gave an embarrassed nod of respect towards my mother and ambled out of the room after my father.

"What do I do, Will?" Meg asked.

I'd never seen tears in those green eyes before that day.

CHAPTER THREE

"Like any devil, he will spare neither man, woman, nor child"

I ran across to where my mother was sitting. She was untangling a silk thread with her fingers, but staring thoughtfully into the fire. "You can see how unfair it is, Mother. *You'll* tell him he can't have Meg hanged."

My mother didn't raise her eyes, but spoke calmly. "I'm sure we'll find a way to help Meg … but talking to your father won't help. He wouldn't raise a finger to help if I asked."

"He's your husband!"

"He married me so that Marsden Manor would have an heir. You were born and I'm no further use to him. He doesn't love me. I don't think he even likes me."

I had never asked questions about my parents: it wasn't my place to ask. But every day I wondered why my mother had ever married a man like Sir James Marsden. Hearing the truth was like the cold shock of diving into the River Wear on a summer day. "So what can we do?"

My mother looked up at Meg and tried to smile. "Your father has given Meg a choice. She must spy on the people in the village, and betray them, or she must die."

"Is there no other way?" Meg asked quietly.

"We could try to find out what really happened to the stolen cup. But, remember, if we do, some other wretch will die. Sir James's pride has been threatened. He wants revenge and he will have it."

"So," Meg said slowly, "I can only stay alive by causing someone else to die."

"Unless Sir James changes his mind. Yes, Meg. That's the choice he's given you."

"It's monstrous," I said.

"He has the law on his side," my mother said. "He doesn't believe he is being cruel or unfair. He believes he is doing good by punishing a sinner."

"You're on his side!" I said.

She looked up at me seriously. "I'm not. I'm just explaining that he's cruel because he is living in a cruel world."

Meg moved forward and sat at my mother's feet. My mother put down her sewing and stroked the girl's wild hair. "What would *you* do?" Meg asked.

"It's not what I would do," my mother said. "It's what I *did* do all those years ago when I was in your position."

"You were accused of theft?" I asked.

"No. Much, much worse. I was accused of *treason*."

"You plotted against Queen Elizabeth?"

"My crime was to be a Catholic in a Catholic family," she explained.

"I never knew you were Catholic," I exclaimed. All my life I'd heard that Catholics were evil and treacherous people who would burn Protestants like me if they ever had the chance. I couldn't believe that my mother was one of those creatures. She had never talked about her family and I realized I knew nothing about them.

She smiled. "I go to our Protestant church every Sunday and I worship as a Protestant. But when I was a child my family secretly worshipped as Catholics. When I was ten years old I was sent away to another family to attend Mistress Yate and be educated. But my family chose

Mistress Yate because they knew that she was a secret Catholic too. All the time I was learning singing, dancing, and writing and counting, I was also learning how to be a good Catholic. I read the Catholic Prayer Book and the Catholic Bible."

"How can you go to a Protestant church now?" Meg asked.

"Because I have learned the truth. It's not the books and the words, or the church and its decorations that matter. It's what's in your heart that matters. I know they would punish me for saying this, Will – so never repeat it – but when I die I don't think God will check to see if I've read the right books. He'll want to know what I've done."

"How will Father answer?" I asked bitterly.

"He will probably tell God he executed people like Meg because the Bible says, 'Thou shalt not steal.' Don't worry. He'll have an answer."

"But you were telling us what happened when you were accused of treason," Meg reminded her.

"It started when I was just a little younger than you, Meg. But I wasn't at all like you. I was quiet and obedient and polite," she said, smiling.

"I try," Meg mumbled.

"No! I didn't mean you are wrong! You've *had* to become strong, Meg. It's not a bad thing. I meant that I was sheltered from the harshness of the world. That's why I wasn't able to cope with what happened to me."

"The treason."

"The treason," Mother nodded. "You have to remember that Queen Elizabeth spent her life hating Catholics. Her sister, Mary Tudor, had burned hundreds of Protestants and she'd even had Queen Elizabeth's godfather, Archbishop Cranmer, burned at the stake. Our queen has never forgotten that."

I shuddered at the thought.

"They tied bags of gunpowder inside their thighs so they would explode and kill the victims quickly. It didn't always work. But it's no worse than what the Protestants are doing to Catholics now," she reminded me.

"True."

"But when I was Meg's age Catholic families like mine and Mistress Yate's were left in peace. We went to the Protestant church on Sunday and we got on quietly with our lives. The Queen knew what was going on, but she didn't try to hound us and destroy us. But she *was* out to destroy the few Catholics who wanted nothing but her death. The ones who were plotting to put Mary Queen of Scots on the throne. They were real traitors. They met with French and Spanish Catholics and tried to arrange for an invasion. They were the people Queen Elizabeth had to uncover."

"So how did you get mixed up with them?" I asked.

"I was at Mistress Yate's house, Lyford Grange, when we had some special visitors. Remember, I was young and I didn't understand everything that was going on in the house. One day three men arrived and were taken straight to the upstairs rooms. They didn't eat with the family and

were never mentioned at the dinner table, but we all knew they were there. One of Mistress Yate's daughters told me that the oldest visitor was a famous Catholic called Campion, although I'd never heard of him."

"Didn't you ask about them?" Meg said.

"You learned never to ask questions like that," Mother explained. "Then on the first Sunday, we went across to the chapel and saw the three strangers dressed in priests' robes. They held a Catholic service for us. They had come directly from the Pope to lead England back to the Catholic Church. I was terrified when I heard what they were saying. Master and Mistress Yate were smiling! I'd no idea they were in so deep. I was so innocent ... or maybe I was just stupid."

"They could have arrested you just for listening to the priests, couldn't they?"

"Of course they could! The punishment was a year in prison and a fine. I couldn't sleep for three nights thinking about it. Then, on the fourth night, there was the noise of horsemen in the courtyard and people running through the house. Someone was hammering on the door with the hilt of a sword. Everyone was dragged from their beds by soldiers and made to line up in the main hall. The servants, the children … everyone except the priests. There were soldiers searching the house for them while we were questioned by two men."

"The Queen's men?"

"One was the Queen's Secretary of State himself, Sir Francis Walsingham. He was the most frightening person I'd ever seen. Tall and thin with a face so sunken it was like looking into a living skull. He was dressed in dark clothes with a black skullcap on his head. And I was small, remember. Looking up I could just see his beard resting on top of his ruff. It looked to me as if his head was being carried round on a plate. His eyes seemed to look clear through me."

"He was Queen Elizabeth's chief spy, wasn't he?" I said.

"That's right. And he had a greasy little fox-faced man with him. That was the Queen's priest-hunter. His name was George Eliot, but it seems everyone called him 'Judas'. All the people at Lyford Grange refused to say they had seen any priests, but 'Judas' Eliot smirked and said his informers had told him they were here. The Queen made sure that informers got a rich reward, you see. Eliot said he'd find the priests if he had to take the house apart stone by stone and panel by panel. It took them just an hour. They found the priests in a secret hiding place underneath the stairs and brought them into the hall. That was when Sir Francis Walsingham walked along the line of people and stared at each one. At last he reached me and stopped."

"You must have been terrified," Meg said.

"I was, and the trouble was I couldn't hide my fear. He could see I was the youngest and the weakest. I nearly fainted when he stretched out a hand and gripped my shoulder. Then he led me to a room nearby and locked the door. There was no light and I sat in the darkness for an age. I tried praying aloud, but my lips were trembling too much and my mouth too dry. When he finally opened the door it was almost daylight outside. That's when the questions started."

"Questions about the priests?" I said.

"He told me he knew everything. He said that Master Yate had told the truth. I was so relieved! I couldn't believe it. I was afraid I'd have to tell lies to save the priests and telling lies would send my soul to Hell when I died. He asked if the men he'd brought in were priests. I said nothing. If I didn't speak, I couldn't betray them – if I didn't speak, then I couldn't lie. He asked me if I'd heard them preach. Again I said nothing. He asked if I was a Catholic and I said nothing. Then he smiled his death's-head smile and called me a good girl. He said I'd have spoken out if they hadn't been priests. He said my silence meant that they *were*!"

"You were really brave," Meg said.

Still my mother shook her head. "I was foolish. I thought my silence would save the men. I should have lied. I should have had the *courage* to lie. My silence did the priests no good. And I showed Secretary Walsingham my fear. That did me no good. It took a few years for Walsingham to use his knowledge of my weakness, but Walsingham was a patient man. At Lyford Grange he'd caught his Catholic traitors. But he was planning for an even greater plot against the Catholics. He'd questioned me and seen how useful I could be to his plans. But I didn't see it!"

I shook my head. "That's no disgrace, Mother," I said. "*I* can't see what his plot could be. How could you have done?"

"I don't know, I don't know. But I should have guessed. He said I'd be free to go home if I promised to be loyal to the Queen and not plot against her. I promised. Then he said he admired me. He said that even if I *was* a Catholic, I was a brave one. Catholics would get to hear of my bravery."

Meg nodded. "That does sound suspicious," she said. "I never trust people when they praise me." Suddenly her hand flew to her mouth. "Except you, madam!"

"I was taken back to my parents. They treated me with respect. They knew that I'd stood up to Secretary Walsingham, and they told me I might have saved the lives of the priests. I felt proud."

"You should be," I told her. "Saving someone's life is a great thing."

"They didn't tell me the truth," my mother sighed. "I was in the garden one day when my father brought in a stranger and sat down to talk. They didn't know I was behind the hedge, and I overheard what they said. I couldn't help it. The stranger said, 'Campion was executed yesterday.' The sound of the words froze me. I would have stepped out, but my father told the stranger, 'Marion must never find out.' Then I couldn't move. I just had to listen to what they said about the executions. It was dreadful."

"What did they say?" I said.

Meg turned to me and answered for her. "They hanged them by the neck till they were almost dead, then cut them down. Then they cut out their bowels and burned them on a fire and then they beheaded them and cut them into quarters."

"I felt *I* did that to them," my mother said. "If I'd been a better liar, Secretary Walsingham wouldn't have seen through me. If I'd thought of a really good lie I could have saved them."

"You couldn't," Meg said.

"Knowing what I'd done nearly broke my spirit. I wanted to die. I wanted to kill myself. But my punishment was to live. I believed that if I lived long enough I would have the chance to redeem myself."

"And you have," Meg said. "I've never met anyone as kind as you."

"And I've never met anyone as sharp as you, Meg. You would never have been bullied by Walsingham."

"You were young."

"But I wasn't so young the second time," my mother sighed.

"A second time?"

"That's right, Meg. You remember I told you I was accused of treason. But it wasn't when I was at Lyford Grange. It was when I was at home and I was fifteen years old. Old enough to know better. Old enough to be taken to the Tower of London on a charge of treason. Lyford Grange was just the start of Walsingham's plot."

Before she had the chance to tell us her story there was a rap on the door and the steward looked into the hall. "Sorry, madam. I was looking for Sir James."

"I think he is in the library."

"Thank you, madam," the man said. He looked behind him into the hallway. "The thing is, madam, there's a man to see Sir James, and I don't like to leave him alone."

"Why not?"

"I don't trust him."

"Then bring him in here and I'll keep an eye on him while you go for Sir James," said my mother.

"Thank you, madam."

"Who is it?"

The steward lowered his voice. "It's Michael the Taverner from the Black Bull. Says he needs to see Sir James urgently. Something about a cup. A silver cup. A stolen cup."

CHAPTER FOUR

"I should rejoice now at this happy news!"

Michael the Taverner was fat. His grey jowls wobbled when he spoke and his red-rimmed eyes never met yours in an honest stare. He pulled off a grey felt hat as he shuffled into the room and bowed to my mother, baring his green teeth in something that was meant to be a smile.

"Good morning, your ladyship," he said. For once his stringy greying hair was combed, he wore a clean, starched yellow ruff over his Sunday-best doublet and he had even shaved.

"Good morning, Master Taverner," my mother said, bowing her head a little. "What a pleasure it is to have a visit from you."

He wrung his hat in his hands the way he twisted his beer-soaked cloths over the filthy floor of the Black Bull. "It's always a pleasure to see you, your ladyship. Your ladyship is the finest lady in the whole county. So gracious, so charming."

My mother glanced at the girl. "Meg was just talking about people who pour praise on you!" she smiled.

A cloud of doubt passed over the taverner's face. "What was she saying?"

"She said she didn't trust them. They usually want something from you."

Michael Taverner threw back his head and laughed, showing rotten black stumps of teeth at the back of his

mouth. "She's a sharp one, that Meg."

"And that's just what I was saying," my mother replied.

The taverner cleared his throat. "If you are ever passing the Bull, you'd be most welcome to call in. I've got a fine Rhenish wine I've just imported from Newcastle."

"I didn't know they made Rhenish wine in Newcastle," my mother said innocently.

"No. They don't. I got the wine from Newcastle, but it came there on a ship."

"Where from?" I asked.

"From where they make the Rhenish wine, Master Will."

"Where's that?" It was cruel to tease the man in this way, but he was one of Marsden Manor's greatest villains and it was no more than he deserved.

"Ah ... oh ... ah ... er, Rhenish-land, of course. Everybody knows that, God's nails! Oh, excuse my language, Lady Marsden. Pardon my language."

My mother raised an eyebrow. "Yes, Michael, we must protect the young people here from strong language. I hope you never speak like that in front of your customers."

"Oh, no! No! No!" he laughed. "The Black Bull is the most respectable tavern in the whole of the north."

"And you called here today, just to invite me to sample your wine," my mother said. "How kind."

"No!" Michael said. "That is – yes. I mean, I would be *honoured* if you would call in one morning." He leaned forward. "It gets a little noisy of an evening," he explained. "Some of the customers become – er – lively."

"Drunk?"

"*Lively.* Noisy. All good, clean fun, you understand. No gambling or swearing!"

"I understand. I will make sure I never visit you in the evening," my mother said. Nor at any other time, I knew.

Michael cleared his throat again. "But the main reason I called was to see Sir James."

"The steward has gone to fetch him."

"Thank you, your ladyship. And, while I am here – and while young Meg is here – I wondered if she had made a decision about working for me. I pay a penny a night."

"But didn't you say your customers were rather rough at night?"

"Lively, I said. Noisy. Nothing Meg couldn't deal with," the man said. "The truth is I need someone to help collect empty pots, make food and serve it, that sort of thing. None of the village women have the time."

The truth was that the village women had all tried and all left the place. He was desperate. If he had to serve beer and food himself, he wouldn't be able to drink with his friends and plot with the other villains who used his tavern as a thieves' meeting place. He knew Meg was tough enough to survive the late hours, the work and the insults. She was also popular with the people in the district.

"We were discussing it when you arrived," my mother said.

"There'll be tips. Some of the customers can be very generous," he went on.

"Meg should be able to give you an answer tonight," Mother said, lowering her voice. "She is in a little trouble with Sir James at present."

"Thank you, your ladyship," the man said and bowed again.

My father walked in and strode across to the table. He sat behind it as if he were at his bench in court. "What do you want?" he demanded.

"Sir James," said the taverner, "you and I have never been the best of friends."

"Maybe because I am the guardian of Her Majesty's law in this part of Durham. You, on the other hand, do everything you can to break the Queen's law, to cheat and steal, to aid and abet cheaters and stealers, to destroy every effort I make to keep the peace. You and I have never been the best of friends, Taverner, and it may be something to do with your criminal ways."

"I have never been convicted of any crimes, Sir James," the man said carefully.

"That is because I have never caught you, or never found anyone brave enough to give evidence against you. But I will, Taverner, I will."

"I am prepared to let bygones be bygones, Sir James. I am ready to forgive you."

My father's face turned a dangerous shade of purple. "You! You forgive *me*! You – what do you forgive me for, you villain?" he exploded.

"Why, for all your suspicions and your accusations, Sir James. In return I hope you will forgive me if I have not always been helpful to Constable Smith when he came round with his interfering questions."

"What do you want, Taverner?" my father snapped.

"I want to extend the hand of friendship," he said,

taking a step closer to my father and holding out his grey hat.

My father looked at it with some disgust and said, "I will grasp your hand and shake it firmly, Taverner ..."

"Thank you, sir."

"... when your fat neck is in a noose and your feet are swinging a yard off the ground. That is the only time I will ever touch that tainted hand of yours."

Michael the Taverner managed to look a little hurt. His gaze seemed to be resting on my father's right shoulder. "Oh, Sir James! I am disappointed. I came here in the spirit of friendship to help you. I respect the law, Sir James."

"Like a cuckoo respects a hedge-sparrow's nest."

"I respect the law. I think you are a hard man – I don't deny it. But you are fair. It really hurts me to see the villagers laughing at you behind your back. I tell them you are just doing your job, but still they laugh. But if you won't let me help you ..."

My father's eyes became sharp and he pushed down on the table and rose to his feet. "Who is laughing at me?" he growled.

Michael shook his head. "It would be easier to list the people who are *not* laughing at you, Sir James."

"Why would they want to laugh?"

The taverner licked his lips and looked round at my mother, Meg and me. "The matter of the cup, Sir James."

My father's head turned sharply towards Meg. He stared at her for a moment, then said to my mother, "Would you be so kind as to take the girl out of the room, Marion. This is a legal matter which may have some importance in her case."

As my mother opened the door I turned to follow them. "Not you,

Will. I may need a witness if the matter comes to court."

He pointed to the seat at the table and I walked over to it. "What do you know about the cup?" I asked.

"I will ask the questions, Will," my father snapped. He turned towards the fat taverner who was sweating now, although we were a long way from the fire and the room was cool. "Now, Taverner, what do you know about the theft of the cup?"

"Oh, I know nothing about the *theft*. All I know is that it was stolen. Right from under the nose of the north's toughest magistrate. You can see why people are laughing."

"But you know that Meg had nothing to do with the theft, don't you?" I demanded.

Michael Taverner flapped a hand helplessly and refused to look me in the eye. "I said, I know nothing at all about the robbery *itself*. I only know that the cup has gone."

"How do you know?" my father asked.

"Gossip in the Black Bull, Sir James. Gossip."

"And do the gossips tell you who stole it?"

"No, Sir James."

"So why are you bothering me with this visit?"

"Because I may be able to point you in the direction of someone who will help you get it back, Sir James."

"You can? Who?"

"I cannot give you the name until you give me a promise, Sir James," the taverner said.

"Why not?"

"This *person* – this person who can help you. She may have to use a little *magic* to help her find it."

"That's against the law!"

"Exactly my point, Sir James! You can see my difficulty? If the woman uses magic, she may be able to tell you where the thief has hidden the cup. But it would be terribly unfair if you got the cup back and then arrested her – or had her hanged for witchcraft."

"Can this soothsayer also tell me who stole the cup?" said my father.

"Ah, no, Sir James. Her magic centres on the object. She can sense where things are hidden. She can't tell who *put* them there."

"Pity."

"Indeed, Sir James."

"What does the woman want out of this?"

"The reward you are offering for the return of the cup. It's worth five pounds – so it's usual to offer a reward of ten shillings."

"How do you know it's worth five pounds?" I asked.

His eyes slid across to my shoulder. "That's what the gossips say."

"And what do you want out of it?"

"Perhaps Sir James would like to make me a little gift of a crown for all the effort I've made to stop him being laughed at."

"How much?"

"Well, then. Let's say a shilling."

"Let's say a shilling," my father agreed sourly. "That's not much for all this *effort* you've made."

The taverner sidled over to the table and rested a dirty hand on it. He leaned forward and spoke quietly. "The woman is very clever, Sir James. Once people hear that she's found your cup, they will come from miles around to buy her services. If they all pay her rewards, then she will become rich. A little of the richness may rub off on to me. She will work from the tavern and I will have more customers. So, you see, Sir James, you will get your cup, the villagers will stop laughing at you, the woman will be rewarded for her powers and I may make an honest penny out of it too. The thief will lose his prize and the other thieves in the area will stay away from Marsden Manor. Everyone is happy."

"I would have the safest manor in the country," my father muttered to himself. He looked up. "Who is this woman?"

"Ah, I need your promise first, Sir James."

My father turned to me. "Your pen and ink are still here, Will. Write down a pardon. Now, Taverner, I'll need her name for the pardon."

"It's Mary, sir, but most people call her Moll."

"Second name?"

"Frith, sir, though she sometimes goes by the name of Markham."

"Let's call her Moll Frith, shall we? Write this, Will: 'I, Sir James Marsden, do hereby pardon Moll Frith of the crime of soothsaying in exchange for information that the afore-said Frith will offer in restoring stolen property to its rightful owners.' Now, pass it to me, Will, and I'll sign it."

I did as he asked, dried the ink and passed the pardon across to Michael the Taverner. "If you will come to the Black Bull tomorrow morning, Moll will try to find your cup for you, Sir James." The man backed towards the door, smirking. He bowed as he slid out.

My father was more excited than I'd ever seen him.

"The safest manor in the county," he chuckled, rubbing his hands together. "The safest manor in the county! This could be the best thing ever to happen to Marsden Manor. This woman will put a stop to Lord Birtley's boasting. Of course we won't tell *him* how we solve our crimes and why the thieves will be flocking into *his* manor. He'll *have* to start hanging them then, won't he?"

"But this means *Meg* won't have to hang, doesn't it?" I asked.

He looked at me, surprised. He blinked in astonishment. "God's teeth, boy, of course it doesn't. The crime was *stealing* the cup. Whether I get it back or not makes not a jot of difference. The girl stole the cup and handed it to some helper. Why, this soothsayer Moll may even find the cup hidden somewhere in the servant girl's room! Don't you understand the first thing about the law, boy? Meg will hang anyway." He marched to the door and swung it open. He looked back at me. "Unless, of course, she agrees to act as my spy in the Black Bull."

I looked down at my right hand. The quill I had been holding was crushed to pieces.

CHAPTER FIVE

"And torture him with grievous lingering death"

Meg looked up brightly and asked, "Does this mean I'm safe?"

She was sitting in the long gallery with my mother. The weak winter daylight made their faces pale and fragile. Portraits of the Marsden family looked down gloomily like a row of stern judges. Meg was sitting in a window seat with my mother, looking at a horn-book, a paper containing the letters of the alphabet and numbers protected by a thin plate of horn. I'd used it myself when I was learning to read.

"Father wouldn't be very pleased if he saw you learning to read, Meg."

"I know," she said. "He says servants don't need to read."

"He also says no woman needs to read," I reminded her.

My mother spoke in the curious sharp way that Father did, sounding just like he did. "A woman's job is in the home. Cooking and cleaning, spinning and weaving. A woman needs to know about herbs and spices and brewing and baking. A woman's place is in the kitchen and the dairy and the sick room, not the library. A woman's work is with bantam cocks and bees and beds and brooms – not books!"

Meg covered her mouth with a hand to smother a giggle. She looked up at me, but saw that I was not smiling. "Oh, Master Will. Don't say you agree with him."

"No."

"Then why are you so miserable?"

"Because he hasn't changed his mind about your spying for him in the Black Bull," I told her.

"Ah," Meg said, dropping her shoulders.

"We still need a plan, then," my mother said.

"I suppose I'll just have to do it," Meg said. "What happened when you became a spy? Michael the Taverner arrived before you could tell us."

"It's a long story," my mother said. "And I'll have to prepare dinner in half an hour. But I can tell you how it happened to me. It's something that Will's grandfather calls black-meal or black-mail."

"That's right," I agreed. "Do what you are told or else. The cattle farmers on the Scottish Borders suffer from black-mailers."

"You remember I told you how the priest Campion was caught at Lyford Grange? I went back to my family as some sort of Catholic heroine and we went on worshipping in the same way. But in 1585, when I was fifteen years old, the Queen and Secretary Walsingham had become more worried by the Catholic traitors. There had been a plot to kill Elizabeth and put Mary Queen of Scots on the throne. So the government made new laws to make it more dangerous to be a Catholic. Priests had forty days to get out of the country and would be executed if they returned. And people sheltering priests were guilty too. Then one day we had a visitor."

"It was a priest, wasn't it?" Meg asked. "It was Lyford Grange all over again. He'd come to ask you to hide him!"

"No, Meg, it wasn't a priest," said my mother.

I was secretly pleased that Meg was wrong – just for once.

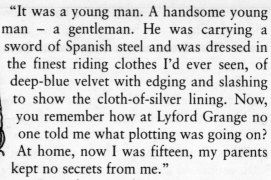

"It was a young man. A handsome young man – a gentleman. He was carrying a sword of Spanish steel and was dressed in the finest riding clothes I'd ever seen, of deep-blue velvet with edging and slashing to show the cloth-of-silver lining. Now, you remember how at Lyford Grange no one told me what plotting was going on? At home, now I was fifteen, my parents kept no secrets from me."

"But what was he?" Meg demanded, bouncing on the cushion of the window seat.

"He was a spy," I guessed. "One of the Queen's spies."

"He was a spy. And he was on his way to the Queen. But he wasn't going to Queen Elizabeth. He was going to Mary Queen of Scots."

"A traitor!" I gasped.

"Sir Francis Walsingham would have called him a traitor," she agreed. "My parents were simple, honest Catholics. They wanted to be free to worship in the Catholic Church. They didn't want the blood of Queen Elizabeth on their consciences. And that was what our visitor Gilbert Gifford was plotting. He was carrying letters to Queen Mary in Tutbury in Staffordshire. They were letters from Spain offering to help Queen Mary to escape and to assassinate Queen Elizabeth."

"What did he want from your family?" I asked.

"Oh, he simply wanted shelter and food for the night, and his friends had told him that we were a loyal Catholic family who wouldn't betray him. They had even mentioned that I was so brave I had stood up to Secretary Walsingham himself. Gilbert Gifford was very impressed by that. He was very interested in meeting me, he said."

"And he was handsome?" Meg asked.

My mother's pale cheeks turned a touch pink as she admitted he was good-looking. "But there was something about his mouth that made him look just a little weak. He said some very flattering things about my face and my figure, but he spoke more like a poet than a real man talking to a real young woman. And, of course, we were never left alone together. Father was very strict about that. My father was a blunt man – he didn't like fancy speaking and he didn't like Gilbert Gifford or his message."

"Treason and murder?" I asked.

"Exactly. Gilbert said that Mary Queen of Scots was a saint. We'd all be rewarded in heaven if we set her free and gave her Queen Elizabeth's throne. Father argued with him for hours over dinner until Gilbert gave up and said that the plot against Queen Elizabeth would be supported by all good Catholics. He said that if Father didn't want to help, he would lose the respect of every Catholic in the country. Father was furious and told Gilbert he could leave the next morning. But by then it was too late."

"You'd already given shelter to a traitor," I said.

"Exactly," my mother said. "I remember that morning well. It was February and there was a sharp frost, just like today. My parents, my brothers and sisters gathered in the courtyard to say goodbye to our guest. My father was as cold as the morning air, especially when Gilbert kissed my hand. Gilbert rode to the gate and waved. By the time he turned back to the road there were three soldiers standing in the gateway. They had pistols pointing at him."

"He was arrested?" I said.

"Oh, Will, we were *all* arrested. Even the youngest children. One of my brothers was only four years old. We were taken over the frozen roads all the way to London. The worst thing was that the soldiers wouldn't tell us where we were going or what we were being charged with. It was only when we reached London that we realized we were heading for the Tower."

"That's where they torture people and execute them," Meg said, shuddering.

"Only the important ones, Meg. Only the traitors. We weren't being treated like ordinary criminals. We were being treated like the most dangerous villains in England. We rode past the end of London Bridge where they have the heads of executed traitors hanging as a warning. One of the soldiers made a joke about our heads looking good up there. Gilbert Gifford almost fainted and fell off his horse when he heard that!"

"What about you, madam?" Meg asked. "You must have been afraid."

"I was more sad for my little brothers and sisters," Mother replied. "They had nothing to do with treason or plots, but they would be questioned, just as I had been at Lyford Grange as a child. I didn't have much time to worry about dying. The people in the streets could see where we were heading. They could see the guards. The people started to follow us, calling names and throwing horse muck at us. The hatred in their faces! Murderers,

they called us. Our guards just laughed and didn't try to stop some boys who tore at my dress with their daggers and spat at me. So you see, Meg, I know how it feels to be found guilty before you're even brought to trial."

Meg nodded. "But you got free. You're here now."

"We did. But the cost was terrible. *You'll* be free if you spy on the villagers in the Black Bull. I went free because I agreed to spy on my fellow Catholics," she said.

"Did they have to torture you to make you do that?" I asked.

"Not exactly. When we reached the White Tower I saw Sir Francis Walsingham waiting for me. He looked ill and greyer and thinner than ever. And I knew that, in our party of ten, it was me he was looking at. He walked straight over to me and helped me down from the saddle. His hand was like a falcon's claw over my wrist. 'Welcome, Miss Marion,' he said. 'I always felt we would meet again one day.' I didn't reply so he went on, 'I hope you have more to say to me than you had at Lyford Grange – or are you still shy?' I hated his voice. So calm. He could send people to their deaths with that same soft tone. No feeling, no mercy."

"Like Father," I said.

"That's unkind. Your father is accidentally cruel. Sir Francis *enjoyed* making people afraid. Because people who are afraid would do what he wanted. He enjoyed the power he had over people."

"Like Father," I repeated.

This time my mother didn't argue. "He said he hoped I wasn't too tired after my journey because he wanted to show me round my new home. My family were led off to their cells while Gilbert Gifford and I were taken to a tower over by the west wall. Secretary Walsingham led us through a small doorway that led into a dark passage. It was damp in there and our feet echoed on the stone floors.

He used a lantern to light the way past barred doors and up twisting stairs. The lantern gave light for him to see his way. But Gilbert and I were left stumbling behind."

"At least you had Gilbert to help," Meg said.

My mother raised an eyebrow. "Gilbert was as much help as one of the rats that ran over my feet. He was badly frightened and too worried about his own safety to worry about me. He held a handkerchief over his nose. The smell was foul. It was the smell of death. I've never known anything like it. Of course, Walsingham kept it that way to terrify his prisoners before they even reached the cells upstairs."

"What were they?"

"The torture chambers," my mother said.

"I thought you said they didn't torture you."

"I said they didn't *exactly* torture me. I mean, they didn't put me on the rack and stretch me. But there are other ways to frighten people into giving in. Walsingham just showed us round the chambers. There was the rack, of course. He called it the Duke of Exeter's daughter after the man who brought it to the Tower – a little joke among the jailers. He said we could be tied, hands to one end and feet to the other, and the ropes pulled till our joints cracked and our limbs were torn out of them. He showed us irons glowing red in fires and explained how they

would be used to burn us. He showed us beams that we would be hung from and thumbscrews that would shatter our hands. He showed us cages that we would be crushed in and the icy water that would be thrown over us. And when he had finished showing us his chamber of horrors he led us to a warm quiet room along the corridor. That's when he told us he was going to let us go."

Meg nodded slowly. "Just like Sir James. Tells me he'll hang me, then says he'll let me go ... if I'll work for him."

"That's right," my mother said. "I was frightened, but Gilbert Gifford was panicking. He'd vomited into his handkerchief and his hands were shaking so much he couldn't drink the warm wine that Sir Francis offered us."

"I can see how Gifford would make a useful spy," I said. "But what use did Walsingham have for *you*, Mother?"

"That was the cleverest part of his plot," my mother said. "And, remember, he'd been planning it for five years, ever since the arrests at Lyford Grange. I was the most important part of the plot. I was the one who was going to make sure that a queen died."

"He wanted you to spy on Mary Queen of Scots," Meg said.

"And betray every Catholic in the country," my mother reminded her. "What would you do?"

Meg gave a weak grin. "That's not fair. I asked first. I asked what you did when you were black-mailed into spying."

I agreed. "Meg needs to know, Mother. She has to decide soon. What did you do?"

My mother rose and looked out on to the frozen trees that kept the weak sunlight off the frozen garden of Marsden Hall. "I told Sir Francis Walsingham that I would spy for him. I gave in."

"And that's what I have to do?" Meg asked.

My mother turned. "I think you have to tell Sir James that you will do it. But remember, I didn't do it alone. I had Gilbert Gifford to help me, but, because he was weak, everything turned out badly for me."

"Right!" Meg said. "I'll do it alone. Better than with some useless man to get in the way."

"No." My mother placed her hands on the girl's shoulders. "I think you should have a man to help you. But one who is clever, brave and cares about you ... not like Gilbert Gifford."

"I don't know any clever men," Meg said with a frown. "In fact I've always thought there's no such thing as a clever man!"

"Then let's just look for a *brave* man who cares for you," said my mother.

Meg shook her head very slowly and wisely. "Can't imagine where I'll find one of those."

"I wonder where we could look?" Mother said.

"Under a stone?" Meg suggested.

"All right!" I cried. "Stop it! Both of you!"

Two pairs of innocent eyes turned towards me and looked at me with mock surprise. "Stop what, Will?"

"Stop this game," I said. "I'll go – I'll look after Meg."

Meg scratched her head and thought about this for a moment. "No, Will. You can come along with me – but *I'll* look after *you*!"

CHAPTER SIX

"Desperate thieves, all hopeless of their lives!"

When I was a child I'd watched some men pull down a barn on a manor farm. When they started to dig foundations for the new barn they uncovered a rats' nest. The tunnels went in every direction with two exits for every entrance; rats scurried round in their own filth and the stuff they'd stolen from the barn.

The Black Bull Tavern in Marsden Village always reminded me of that rats' nest. It was a maze of corridors and little rooms with doors and stairways where you least expected them. It was also filthy and full of stolen hoards. Michael the Taverner and his customers were the rats. Hard-working, scurrying round at their thieving life and coming out only in the dark. My father was right, for once, when he said that the Black Bull was the centre of all the crime in our manor. If I ever took over the manor, I decided, I would level it to the ground and drive the rats out to find a new nest somewhere else.

Getting Meg into the rambling red-brick tavern had been easy enough. But it took a long time for us to work on *my* disguise. We agreed that I was going to be her cousin from Wearmouth and that I was a beggar. "You are deaf and dumb," said Meg. "That way your voice won't give you away."

She was holding my disguise in front of the kitchen fire to dry. Meg had explained that she could take some of my old clothes and exchange them for the rags of a beggar who lived in Birtley. It seemed like a good idea until I saw the rags. The lice were crawling over them and the fleas were jumping in black clouds. "I can't wear those!" I cried.

"I'll wash them to get rid of the worst of your little friends," she offered.

"And wash out the smell!" I said.

"Yes, but not *too* much of the smell. You need to smell if you're going to be a beggar."

I groaned. "Can't I be a clean beggar?"

"No such thing. Even clean beggars make themselves *look* dirty and pathetic so people feel sorry for them. Don't you know anything? And while we're making you look dirty, we really should give you a few sores that weep pus through the bandages. They always look good."

I felt a little sick at the thought. "You can't *give* people sores," I said.

"Of course you can!" she laughed. "Palliard beggars do it all the time. They just take crowfoot and spearwort and salt and bind them on to the skin till it comes out in a rash. Then you wrap a cloth round the rash till it sticks to the wound. When you pull the cloth off you have a raw hole in your flesh. Sprinkle on a little rat poison to make it look really bad, then you're ready to beg. I could do it for you if you like."

"No, thank you."

"Why not?"

"Because there isn't time."

"Ah! I thought it might be because you haven't the courage."

I ignored that comment. "And another thing," I said. "If my father catches me, he'll have me whipped. His job as magistrate is to have all beggars whipped if they haven't got a licence."

"He wouldn't whip his own son," Meg objected.

I looked at her solemnly.

"You're right," she grinned. "He would!"

Meg turned back to the fire and checked the clothes. "They're nearly dry," she said. "A bit of dampness in the freezing air outside and you'll be shivering and pathetic just like a real dummerer."

"What's that?"

"A beggar who pretends to be deaf and dumb."

"Except, if other beggars question us, you tell them I really *am* dumb. Yes?"

"Yes."

"I hope I can do this," I muttered as I took the dirty rags from her.

"You want to be an actor, don't you? Well, now's your chance to practise. Take your drawers off."

"What?"

"Your drawers. You may wear fine linen under your hose. Beggars wear nothing. Take them off."

"Me-eg!" I wailed. "I'll be cold."

"Take them off."

"These rough clothes will rub me raw."

"Good. That's the idea. Take them off."

"But ..."

"Off!"

"Look the other way."

"Hah!" She sniffed and turned to throw wood on the fire while I took off my clothes and put on the rags. They were too big and the fastenings were broken, so I had to clutch them round me.

Meg swept some cinders into a pile at the edge of the hearth and took some cool ones and ground them between her hands. She rubbed the dust into my hair, my face and my arms and legs where they showed through the rags. She used a charred log to add blackened patches

under my eyes and between my toes. "No one will see my feet. I'll be wearing shoes," I told her.

"No you won't."

"It's icy out there, Meg. My feet will freeze!"

"I know. It must be a terrible life, being a beggar." The teasing sparkle in her eyes vanished for a moment as she added, "But at least you have Marsden Hall to come back to when your acting is over."

"I know."

"And if Michael the Taverner suspects who you really are, then you'll have more to worry about than frozen toes," she reminded me. "Now, let me look at you – yes. I've done a wonderful job. Let's hope your acting is half as good."

She opened the kitchen door and my naked feet crunched over the frozen spikes of the kitchen garden. It hurt as I hobbled towards the small gate in the high wall that surrounded Marsden Hall. The wheel ruts in the road were frozen into knife blades under my feet and the icy crust on puddles broke and sent a chill up my legs that crept through my whole body.

It was late afternoon and the heavy sky was filled with rooks screaming as they teemed home to Bournmoor Woods to roost for the night. Villagers were hurrying home from work in the fields. They bent their heads into the cold wind and pretended they couldn't see the dummerer stumbling towards them.

I pulled the stinking hood over my head as we entered the front door of the Black Bull Tavern and stepped into the main room. The air was suddenly hot and thick with tobacco smoke that mingled with the smoke from rush lights. The noise battered my ears like a blow from a hand. The room was full of men and women all turned towards a space that had been cleared in the middle of the room. They were clapping and cheering and slamming tankards on to the tops of the tables.

We pushed our way through the crowd to see what was happening. It was a tumbler performing acrobatics and dancing wildly to a fiddler's tune. The tumbler was heavily built, but light on his feet. His yellow hair was a blur as he tumbled and leapt across the floor. He dived forward on to his hands and flipped his legs over his head till he landed on his feet again. When he staggered into the circle of watchers they roared with laughter and cheered. He cartwheeled back across the room and swung round in a fast spin.

Then his voice boomed out in a song as the fiddle screeched and tried to follow the tune. It was something about a young woman who lost her lover and killed herself. Still, the audience didn't seem to mind the miserable story. They joined in the last two lines and roared out the words: *Oh, love is pleasing, and love is teasing, and love is a pleasure when first it is new. But as it grows older, it waxes colder, then fades away like the morning dew!*

The performer bellowed the last chorus, then staggered back to a seat at a table while the watchers cheered and cried for more.

"Landlord! More ale!" the dancer cried.

"More ale!" the crowd joined in.

"I only have two pairs of hands!" Michael the Taverner shouted angrily.

His customers screeched with laughter and he jabbed a filthy finger at them. "One pair of hands, then. You know what I mean!"

Suddenly he caught sight of Meg and called, "Here, girl! Take this wine across to Moll."

"Who?"

"The lass who's just been singing and dancing."

"It's a woman?" Meg asked.

"Of course it's a woman. She looks a bit rough, but believe me, Moll is a woman."

Meg nodded over her shoulder. "My cousin here is deaf and dumb. My aunt asked me to look after him."

"Put him in the far corner," Michael said with a half glance in my direction. "Keep him out of sight of the customers. He'll put them off their food and drink."

I nearly gave an angry reply, but remembered I was deaf and dumb. As Meg pushed her way across to Moll's table with a flagon of wine I followed her and squeezed down behind the dancer. I sat on the floor with my back to the wall. Now that she was sitting still I could see that she was a woman. She wasn't very old, probably less than twenty. She spoke with a strange accent that I thought might be the way London people talked. Her figure was solid enough to be a man's, and a strong man at that. She sucked at a pipe between gulps of wine straight from the flagon and snatches of conversation with her admirers, who crowded round the table and almost trampled on my bare feet.

At last she had spoken to everyone and the crowd began to thin as they moved away to find drinks and bowls of Michael Taverner's greasy chicken stew. I could

see Meg hurrying back and forth from the barrels of ale on a bench beside the landlord to the customers at the table.

Meg was working so hard she would have had few chances to spy, but from my position behind yellow-haired Moll I could see and hear a lot. When Michael was satisfied that Meg could serve and take the customers' money he waddled across the room and sat down next to Moll. He spoke quietly, but seemed to believe Meg's story that I was deaf as well as dumb because he saw me, yet made no effort to move me.

"Moll," he said, "I have a customer."

"You have fifty customers tonight, Master Taverner. I hope you don't run out of wine and ale."

"I mean I have a customer for you and your soothsaying skills."

I jumped and almost showed too much interest in their talk. I buried my head between my knees and pretended to sink into an exhausted sleep. So, this was Moll Frith the soothsayer who was going to find our stolen silver cup. It would be interesting to see how she did it.

She was drinking huge amounts of wine, but it seemed to have no effect on the sharpness of her speech and her eye. "What is it?"

"The silk dress taken from a house at Penshaw last Friday."

"I know the one," Moll said. "Who's the owner?"

"Master Gregory," Michael Taverner said.

"He must be a funny shape to fit into that red silk dress!" Moll said. She threw back her head and roared with laughter.

"It's his *wife's* dress," Michael said, not seeing that it was a joke.

"Is it really?" Moll replied. "You surprise me, Master Taverner. What is it worth?"

"Master Gregory says it's worth four guineas, but I think he is trying to save on paying the reward. Let's say it's worth ten pounds."

"Let's say that, shall we, my fat friend?" Moll agreed.

Michael looked uncomfortable at the insult. He tightened the leather thong round his apron to pull in his belly, then sidled across to a side door. A thin, hawk-faced man came into the room, his nostrils pinched with disgust. His wife was even thinner. She looked terrified at the sight of so many noisy, drunken people gathered in one room.

In a single movement Moll had tied a black handkerchief round her head. She swept a book from the floor and placed it in front of her on the table. Her round, smiling face had become serious and her shapeless body was pulled up straight on the bench. She spread both arms wide and said in a hoarse voice, "Sit, my friends!"

Master and Mistress Gregory sat facing Moll and I risked a quick glance up at them. They were sitting forward like a pair of greyhounds waiting to be fed. Moll suddenly stretched out a hand. As if they were tied together, the Gregories jumped. Moll gave a low moan of misery. "Ohhhh! Ohhhh! The pain! The pain! I can feel that you two have suffered."

Master Gregory nodded. "We have!"

"Suffered," Mistress Gregory agreed.

"A loss!" Moll groaned. "A loss of something worth ten pounds or more!"

"Well, five pounds, anyway," Master Gregory nodded.

"Or maybe even eight!" his wife added.

"You may have paid eight for it, but now it's worth ten," insisted Moll.

"She could be right," said Mistress Gregory.

"Perhaps."

"I see a pope!"

"We're not Catholics!" Master Gregory squawked. "Never have been! Never would be!"

"I see a pope!" Moll said louder. People at surrounding tables were watching her, amused, but the rest of the room was as noisy as ever. "Your names – your names are the names of a pope."

"Pope Gregory!" the woman cried. "We are Mistress and Master Gregory! Amazing!"

"I feel something soft," Moll said, waving her fingers as if she were stroking a cat. "Soft and red. Is it satin?"

"No! It's silk!" said Master Gregory.

"But she's close," Mistress Gregory put in.

"Could it be … a dress?" the soothsayer asked.

"It could!"

"It is!"

"Tell me your birth dates," Moll said quickly.

"He's June the tenth and I'm August the thirty-first," Mistress Gregory said.

"And the dress went missing on Saint Valentine's day, last Friday, did it not?"

"How did you know that?" Master Gregory asked.

"Because she knows everything," his wife told him.

Moll suddenly snatched at the book she had placed on the table and riffled through the pages. She held it in such a way that Master and Mistress Gregory couldn't see it, but from my place on the floor I could see diagrams and figures. "The almanac will guide us to your lost dress," Moll told them.

I had seen a book like this before. My tutor had used one to teach me geometry. It was a mathematic book by the Ancient Greek writer, Euclid. It was no more an almanac than I was a beggar!

"Oh, yes-s-s!" Moll hissed. "On Friday the planet Mars was opposed to the planet Venus when the moon was new. Anyone born under the constellation of the Scorpion would suffer terrible loss. Oh, my friends, you are so lucky!"

"You call the loss of a ten-pound dress lucky?"

"It could have been so much worse. Mars is a cruel planet and the loss could have been your lives! Mars is the red planet ... you lost a red dress ... but it could have been red blood I was looking at."

"We have been lucky," Mistress Gregory cried.

"But will we get the dress back?" her husband demanded.

Moll turned a few more pages and looked at some pictures of triangles. "A building of wood and straw is indicated here."

"We have a wooden barn," Master Gregory said.

"With straw inside," his wife put in excitedly.

"Mars is to the north tonight and Venus to the east – look in the north-east corner of the barn and see what you will find."

Mistress Gregory jumped to her feet. "We'll go there right away," she said.

Her husband rose a little more slowly. "But what would it be doing there?"

"Perhaps the thief took it from your house and hid it there, meaning to come back for it later," Moll suggested.

"In that case we'd better hurry," Mistress Gregory said, tugging at her husband's arm.

"What? And maybe meet the rogue who stole it?" he cried. "He may kill us!"

Michael the Taverner had been lingering at a nearby table, pretending to wipe up slopped beer. He turned to the couple and said, "One of my most trusty and sturdy friends could go with you. His name is Wat Grey. Just say, 'What's what, Wat?' He's the bravest and most honest man in England. If there are thieves about you'll be as safe with him as with an army!"

I almost choked when I heard this. Wat was as trusty as a magpie and had a magpie's taste for picking up shiny objects that didn't belong to him.

"You're very kind," Master Gregory said as Wat Grey appeared from across the room in response to a tiny signal from the taverner's eyebrow.

"And, when you've found the dress, you can give honest Wat the twenty shillings reward!" Michael said. "It will save you having to return to the Black Bull tomorrow ... though you are always welcome, of course, Master Pope."

"Gregory."

"As you say. Goodnight, sir, and thank you for your business," the taverner said in the same wheedling voice he used with my father.

"No," Master Gregory said, "thank *you*, Master Taverner."

The happy couple hurried from the room. Moll chuckled, turned and threw the book on the floor where it landed on my foot. I had to bite my lip to stop myself crying out. "Sorry, friend," Moll said. She reached into the purse that dangled from her belt and pulled out a groat. She threw it at me and I caught it. "Have yourself a bowl of Michael's chicken stew!"

Meg came across the room with a bowl of the brown mess and put it in my hands. "Here you are, cousin," she said. "Kind Moll will want to see you eat every last drop!"

Michael Taverner had used every bit of the chicken to make the awful brew. There were pieces of the skin, innards and some of its sinews floating around.

Moll turned up her short nose. "I wouldn't eat that muck myself," she said.

"Ah, but my cousin is a poor beggar," Meg smiled. "He'll eat anything and be so grateful he'll kiss your feet. Won't you, cousin?" She snatched the groat from my hand and replaced it with the bowl. "Eat up!"

I don't think I have ever hated anyone as much as I hated that girl. If I could have spoken I would have told her my father's idea of hanging her was just too kind. Something slow and painful would have been better. As slow and painful as having to eat Michael's chicken stew under the kind gaze of Meg and Moll.

I ate.

CHAPTER SEVEN

"And roughly send to prison the immediate heir of England"

The morning after our visit to the Black Bull was not a pleasant one for me. The journey home at midnight had been even colder and darker and harder on my feet as I stumbled over daggers of ice. I limped down to breakfast next morning, clutching my stomach and trying not to retch.

My mother bathed my feet in witch hazel while my father complained, "You'll make the boy soft, Marion."

"He and Meg did well last night, James. The boy deserves to be looked after," my mother replied mildly.

"Why aren't you eating your breakfast, Will?" my grandmother asked me. "These eggs are delicious."

"Aye," Meg said quietly as she held out the dish to me. "And eggs are just unborn *chickens*. And you do love *chicken*, Master William, don't you?"

I clenched my teeth and said, "Take the eggs away."

She smiled, dropped a curtsey and placed the eggs on the table where Great-Uncle George scooped up my share happily.

"So what exactly did you find out last night?" my father asked.

For the next half hour we told him the story of Moll Frith and her soothsaying powers. "It must have worked because Wat Grey came back later with twenty shillings. He kept five shillings, gave five to Michael the Taverner and ten to Moll," I explained. I didn't tell him Moll was so pleased that she offered to buy me another bowl of stew. That was when I pretended to be asleep.

"Of course, soothsaying is a crime in itself," my father said. "But if it helps us to prevent a greater crime like theft then we can overlook it."

"Soothsaying is also a crime against God," my mother reminded him.

"Ah, well, I'm sure God won't mind too much if I use it to stamp out thieving in Marsden Manor!" he replied. He spoke as if he and God were old and dear friends.

"I look forward to seeing this Moll woman," my grand-mother said. "Maybe she can find the wig I lost twelve years ago come Easter."

"I told you," Grandfather said. "A bird blew off with it to make a nest."

"That's right," Great-Uncle George put in. "Look for a bird with a ginger nest and you'll find the thief!"

Grandmother turned on him. "It wasn't ginger – it was auburn, just like Meg's hair." She and her stepbrother, Great-Uncle George, fought like hound and fox.

"It was as red as a sunset and it looked as if you were wearing a ginger tomcat on your head," the old soldier laughed.

Before Grandmother could reply my father raised a hand. "Mother! Uncle George! Please! I really don't want villagers like Michael the Taverner to come here and see you squabbling like this. If you wish to see this Moll woman working her spells then I will have to ask you to watch quietly."

"There's no harm in asking about my wig," Grandmother said.

"Your ginger tomcat," Great-Uncle George muttered.

"The woman will be here in less than an hour," Father said loudly to prevent any more argument. "Shall we look at the estate accounts?" he asked Grandfather.

The old man rose stiffly and nodded. Grandmother and Great-Uncle George followed them out of the door. "That wig cost me twelve pounds in Newcastle," Grandmother complained. "It's not a laughing matter."

Great-Uncle George just grinned and said, "Miaow!"

When it was quiet again in the hall my mother bound my feet in linen cloth and I slipped on a pair of Great-Uncle George's old boots since they were larger than mine and fitted my swollen, bandaged feet. As Meg cleared the breakfast table my mother took a cup of wine and plunged a poker from the fire into it until the wine spat and bubbled. She added a few herbs from a purse on her belt. "Drink this," she said offering the cup. "It will help your stomach cramps and ease the ache in your feet."

I drank the warm wine and sat heavily in the chair by the fireplace. My mother sat opposite and, when Meg finished her work, she came and sat at her feet.

"So how did you feel about spying, Meg?"

"No one was harmed by it," Meg said carefully. "It might have been different if I'd seen someone commit a crime. If I'd had to report back to Sir James that Moll was a thief, and knew that he would hang her, that would have made it harder."

"It would," my mother sighed.

"You had to do that," Meg said, "didn't you?"

"Yes," said my mother, nodding. "It wasn't a matter of a stolen dress. It was a matter of the life and death of a queen. I could save Queen Elizabeth's life by betraying Mary Queen of Scots – or I could save Queen Mary's life by betraying Elizabeth. It was an awful position for a sixteen-year-old girl to be put in. But Sir Francis Walsingham didn't seem to mind my misery so long as he got what he wanted."

"Would he really have tortured you?" I asked.

"No. I would have been no use to him if I was broken on the rack. He threatened to torture my father and mother. He even said that my little brothers would be interested to see how his torture machines worked."

"But he didn't have that sort of hold over Gilbert Gifford, did he?"

"No," my mother agreed. "He simply told Gifford to work against Queen Mary or die a traitor's death of hanging, drawing and quartering. Gifford didn't need any other threats."

"What did Walsingham ask you to do?"

"To become Queen Mary's lady-in-waiting and to watch her household from the inside. To report any attempt by her to plot against Elizabeth. Remember Gifford had come from France to help Queen Mary. He had to talk to the French spies in London and tell them he had a foolproof plan to get messages in and out of her prison at Tutbury Castle."

"What was the plan?" I asked.

"I'd have used pigeons to carry messages," Meg said.

"Spies *did* use pigeons," said Mother. "But spy-catchers used hawks to catch the pigeons and read the messages wrapped round their legs."

"I suppose a messenger couldn't just ride in and take a letter?" I asked.

"All messengers were stopped by the guard and all messages were read by their commander."

"You'd have to smuggle them in some way," Meg said. "When something was delivered to Tutbury there would be a message inside. A message that only Queen Mary's servants would know about."

"That's very clever, Meg!" my mother smiled.

"It's obvious," I sniffed.

She ignored me and went on, "The guards would search everything that came in. It had to be so well hidden that a guard would never find it."

"You're right," said my mother. "The letters were sealed in packets and hidden in a secret compartment in a beer barrel. The French spies gave the letters to Gifford, and Gifford gave them to Sir Francis Walsingham. Sir Francis read the letters, then gave them back to Gifford. Gilbert Gifford hid the letters in the beer barrels and had them delivered to Tutbury. Queen Mary's servants found them and took them to her."

"And the same thing happened when Queen Mary replied, I suppose. She would hide the letters in the empty barrels when they were sent back to the brewery, Gifford would pass them on to Sir Francis and then they would go back to Gifford to send to the French," I said. "So Queen Elizabeth knew everything that Mary Queen of Scots was writing to the French about."

"She did."

"So why did Sir Francis need you to spy inside the prison?" Meg asked.

"Because," I said, "he needed to know if the plan was working, or if Queen Mary suspected Gifford. And he needed to know if she had any other ways of sending messages to anyone else."

"Very good, Will," my mother said.

"It's obvious," said Meg.

"It was cunning. Secretary Walsingham left nothing to chance. He had a man called Phelippes who was an expert in secret codes. Queen Mary's messages were in a secret alphabet, but Phelippes had worked it out, so it did her no good. The poor lady might as well have shouted her messages from the battlements of Tutbury!"

"Did Walsingham's plan work?" I asked.

"They had to test it before I went to work at Tutbury. After all, Gifford could have lost his nerve and betrayed us all. But Gifford went to the French and said he had a safe message system. The French sent a letter to Queen Mary – which Secretary Walsingham read, of course – and she sent a reply saying that the message had arrived safely. She said that the French could write what they liked because the scheme was watertight!"

"Or beertight," I said with a grin.

Meg and my mother looked at me. They didn't smile. Sometimes I wonder if women have the same sense of humour as men. My mother went on, "Then Secretary Walsingham wrote a letter to Queen Mary. It was in her secret code and was supposed to come from a French supporter. It said there was a good Catholic girl who would like to work for her. He gave my name and explained that I was present when the priest Campion was captured at Lyford Grange five years before. The letter said I was well known as a brave and loyal supporter of the Catholic cause, and that the Queen could trust me with her every secret."

"It was a good lie," Meg said, "because there was a lot of truth in it."

"That's right. Queen Mary's Catholic friends would have heard about me and would tell her to trust me. None of them knew that my family had been taken to London and were being threatened with terrible torture."

"They could have found out," I said.

My mother smiled. "They could," she agreed. "So Secretary Walsingham sent my family home. He said that if *they* betrayed me to their Catholic friends then *I* would die – and he told me that if *I* betrayed Queen Elizabeth my *family* would die. It was a trap. There was no way out that I could see."

"What was it like?" Meg asked. "Going into a prison like that?"

"You have to remember I'd been in the Tower of London, so nothing held any real terrors for me. That was before I saw Tutbury, of course!"

"But Mary was a queen," I said. "They'd have put her in a palace."

"Queen Mary was a *prisoner* and they put her in a fortress," my mother said. "She had been guarded by Queen Elizabeth's jailers for more years than I'd been alive. They had moved her from castle to castle, but Tutbury was the one she hated most. It was more like the ghost of a dead castle. At one time it had been like a walled town, but no one could afford to keep it in good repair. It was patched and mended where it had crumbled, but all the tapestries in the world couldn't keep out the draughts and the bitter winds. And all the colour of the tapestries couldn't hide the greyness and gloom of the old walls."

"Even Marsden Manor's cold in the winter," I said.

"I know, but Tutbury was as bad in every season. It was built on a hill that rose out of a swamp, and the damp rose up from the swamp and chilled every bone in your body. Then there was the choking smell of the swamp. All that rotting weed was even worse in summer. I can understand why Queen Mary hated Tutbury. It was Easter time before she replied and agreed to take me as her lady-in-waiting. When I set off it was a bright spring day, but the smell of the swamp met me five miles from the castle. I couldn't believe the misery of the place as it reached out to clutch at me and pull me in."

"Was it as bad as the Tower of London?" Meg asked.

"Worse. It was frightening, like the Tower, but it had a loneliness about it that made me feel I was riding off the end of this world and into another, much worse place. The guards opened the massive gates for me and I heard them shut behind me with a booming that sounded like the gates of Hell."

"Were you a prisoner too?" I asked.

My mother nodded. "In a way. That first day I met the governor of the castle, Sir Amyas Paulet. He made it quite clear that once I had met the Queen I was no longer free to go where I wanted. He might let me out to visit my family from time to time, but I would always be searched

and always watched. He asked if I wanted to change my mind. I said, 'No.' He must have known that my family's safety depended on it. He told me that he knew I came from Sir Francis Walsingham – but he said I was still a Catholic and *he* would never trust me."

"What was Mary like?" Meg asked.

A voice boomed from the doorway, "You know what she's like! You met her last night, girl!"

I turned to see a broad, yellow-haired figure standing in the doorway. The figure was dressed like a man, but I knew it was the young woman, Moll Frith. "Hello, young Meg!" she cried. "Found a back door open. Let myself in. You don't mind, do you?"

My mother turned a little pale. "I'm Lady Marsden. Who are you?"

"I'm the Mary you were talking about, aren't I? Though my friends call me Moll. Moll Frith's the name and soothsaying's me game."

"Welcome to Marsden Hall, Mistress Frith."

"Call me Moll."

"Welcome to the hall ... Moll."

I stood slightly behind my mother. She placed an arm round my shoulders and said, "This is my son Will."

Moll grinned. Her teeth were strong, but now I could see in the daylight they were stained brown by the tobacco she smoked. "Fine-looking young man," she said. It was clear she didn't recognize me as the grey-faced hooded beggar who'd sat behind her the previous night. "Fine-looking young man! Don't suppose you're looking for a wife, young Will?"

"Not yet."

"Let me know when you are," she said, winking. "I'm your girl. You won't find a harder-working or livelier wife in the world. Why, I can even do acrobatics!"

"I know."

"You what?"

"Er ... I've heard – Meg was just telling us! Weren't you, Meg?"

"I was, I was," the girl said quickly, "and a wonderful dancer."

"That's not all!" Moll said. "I can do magic – real and fake."

"I'll remember that next time we have an entertainment in the grounds of Marsden Hall," Mother said.

"I'm your girl!" Moll boomed, slapping her leg.

Mother turned to Meg and asked her to tell Sir James that his soothsayer was here. She turned back politely to the young woman. "You're not local, are you, Moll?"

"London, Lady Marsden ... or can I call you Marion? Of course, you won't mind. We're all friends here, aren't we?"

"Well ..."

"Anyway, Lady Marion. I was born in London – a wild and dangerous place. You have to be quick with your fists if you live where I lived. Many's the nose I had to break with this here fist! Hah! They tried to teach me needle-work and spinning. But women have such boring lives I wanted nothing to do with it. I ran away to join a theatre company, didn't I?"

"But they don't let women act on the stage," I said. I had seen travelling companies when they had come to Durham and Newcastle, and I knew that all the women's parts were played by boys whose voices hadn't broken.

"They don't let women on the stage, it's true. But I pretended to be a boy, didn't I?"

"Did you?"

"Oh, yes! I said I would play the women's parts for them, didn't I?"

"And they let you?"

"'Course they did. I was very good at playing the part of a woman. That was the joke, see? I was a woman pretending to be a boy who went on stage pretending to be a girl! And sometimes the girl in the play had to pretend to be a boy! So I was a girl pretending to be a boy pretending to be a girl pretending to be a boy!"

"Amazing!" my mother said faintly.

"Amazing indeed. I think you'll find I am a pretty amazing woman."

"But you gave up acting," my mother said.

"Had to, didn't I? I found I had the power of second sight. Anyway, I grew too big to be taken for a boy and too pretty to be anything other than a girl. You can see that, can't you?"

My mother blinked. "Ah! Yes! Much too – er – pretty!"

"You're not so bad yourself, Marion … for your age! When I'm your age I hope I'm as well preserved. And I also hope I have a husband as fine as young Will here. You don't fancy betrothing him to me, do you? We wouldn't marry till he was old enough, of course!"

"I have to admit that you are the first lady to make an

offer for him," my mother said. "I will talk to his father about it tonight after supper."

"You do that, Marion. I'm as good a catch as he's likely to get." She sucked on her pipe and smacked her lips. "Now, then! Where's your Jim?"

"My what?"

"Your husband? He's called Jim, isn't he?"

"Sir James."

"That's what I said. Jimmy. Let's get started, shall we?"

"Let's," my mother agreed.

CHAPTER EIGHT

"The treasure of thy heart"

When my father met Moll Frith he was startled. "I expected someone a little older," he said.

"There you go, Sir Jim!" she said. "That's what they all say. They think witches should be old women with cats or toads or hares to keep them company. But of course, I'm not a witch – otherwise you'd hang me, wouldn't you?"

"I would," my father agreed.

"I'm simply a person who gives information about stolen property. I'm not allowed to charge one groat for my services."

"That's good."

"But *most* people like to give me one pound for every ten pounds the stolen object is worth."

"Ah," my father said, looking disappointed.

"Take me to the place where the object was stolen," Moll demanded.

Father led the way to the kitchen and I followed, leaving Meg and my mother in the hall. In the kitchen the cook was busy scouring out his pans with sand and the kitchen boy was stirring a pot of soup that was bubbling over the fire. It smelled of pork that had been salted and dried since November and would be tender after a day's simmering, and of herbs that I'd helped Grandmother collect from the kitchen garden the previous autumn.

I'd eaten no breakfast and the smell from this pot was

making me hungry. I was recovering from Michael
Taverner's chicken stew of the night before. Moll looked
round at the copper pans and the pewter plates, the shining spoons and the pottery jugs. "There's a lot of valuable
stuff here, Sir Jim," she said.

"Ah, but the family silver is kept under lock and key
upstairs," my father said.

"You have silver, do you?"

"I do. Some of it is very old and special guests admire
it greatly."

"You have special guests, do you?"

"The Earl of Durham and Lord Lambton are regular
visitors," Father boasted. The truth was they called by
once a year.

"And you get your silver out then, do you?"

"I do."

"So how did your silver cup come to be stolen last
Saturday, Sir Jim?"

"One of the servants was given the task of cleaning the
silver. I unlocked the cupboard and gave her a cup. She
brought it down to the kitchen here to get cleaning rags
and sat at this table."

"I see," Moll said.

There was a slow change coming over the young woman. I'd seen it in the Black Bull when Master and Mistress Gregory had come to meet her. Her body went stiff and her eyes wide and staring. Her voice grew lower as if she were afraid of being overheard.

"I knew the thief took the cup from this table," she repeated. "I knew it before you even told me!"

"That's amazing," my father breathed, lowering his voice to match hers.

"As you know, an animal doesn't have a soul, otherwise this kitchen would be haunted by the spirits of the sheep and cattle and pigs you've eaten," Moll explained.

"Of course," Father said. "In olden times the Catholics would have burned you for saying that animals had souls."

"They would," Moll agreed. "But everything has its own place in the universe – the stars, the moon, the mountains and the rivers, right down to the stones in the road."

"Yes," my father said, trying to follow her argument.

"And your silver cup has its place. That place is here in this house. Now it has gone, it is out of its place. It is lost. It is lonely. It is a poor little cup crying out to be back where it belongs. Can you hear it, Sir Jim?"

My father screwed up his face and strained to listen. "No," he said.

"No," said Moll sadly. "You don't have my skill. But even you can hear all the rest of your silver crying out for their lost friend, can't you?"

My father's eyes narrowed. The cook and the kitchen boy had stopped work and even I was straining to hear. My father said, "I do believe I can hear something!"

"Of course you can," Moll said. "Let's go and see your silver goods, shall we? See if they can help us to find their lost partner!"

My father opened a door that led to a back stairway. It wound its way upward and led out on to the upstairs landing. Moll followed as he led the way to a cupboard set deep in the wall. He selected a key from the ring on his belt and put it in the lock. It opened smoothly and he pulled the door open. Inside it was gloomy, but the silverware shone brightly. There were cups and plates and a huge silver salt dish in the shape of a ship in full sail. That caught Moll's eye. "That's a fine piece of silver, Sir Jim!"

"It's been in the family for two hundred years or more," he said, stroking the smooth metal sails as if they were a favourite cat. "It's priceless."

"I can imagine," Moll said. "I can see why you keep it locked away."

"No thief could sell it even if it were stolen," my father said, with a smug smile. "There is no other salt-holder exactly like it in the world. The thief who tried to sell it would be caught as soon as he took it into a silversmith."

"That's true," Moll sighed. "Stealing's easy. Getting rid of stolen property for a fair price is a difficult business."

"Is it?"

"So they tell me."

"So my silver salt-ship is safe," Father nodded.

"Well ... I guess the thief could always pound it with a hammer till it was just a block of solid silver," Moll suggested.

Father gasped. "This is a work of art!"

"It's warm clothes and hot meals for some poor prigger!" Moll said.

"No prigger would get my silver," Father said.

"Some prigger *did* get your cup," she reminded him.

"Only because they had inside help," he snarled. "It will not happen again." He swung the door shut and turned to the young woman. "Now, what have my calling cups been shouting about their lost friend?"

"What's your birth date?"

"What?"

"Your birth date! The day you were born!"

"I know what a birth date is. I just don't see what it's got to do with my lost cup."

"It's all to do with your horoscope, Sir Jim! The more I know about the forces in this house the more I'll be able to help!"

"I was born on the ninth of September," he said.

"What time?"

"Five in the morning."

Moll placed her hands on the door to the silverware cupboard and closed her eyes. "I feel cold, so cold."

"You could come and sit by the fire in the hall," Father suggested.

"I am drowning!"

"What?" my father asked.

"I think she's imagining she's the cup," I said. "It isn't Moll that's cold, it's the cup!"

"I see! Amazing!"

"Water. I see water. Running water. Cold water. A river."

"My cup has been dumped in a river!"

"No. It has been left there so the thief can come back and claim it when it's safe."

"Is is the River Wear? The river at the far side of Bournmoor Woods?"

"Yes. Woods. Carried through woods. Past a cottage."

"That'll be Widow Atkinson's cottage," said Father.

"A bridge! I'm falling off a bridge. And then cold water. So cold!"

"It must be at the edge where the thief can just reach a hand into the water and pick it out," I said.

"You're right, Will," he said. "I had thought of that myself." He cleared his throat. "Thank you, Mistress Frith! That was very interesting."

Moll turned to face us. Her eyes were rolling upwards and she took a minute to fix them on us. She looked surprised to see us. "Did I say something?"

"You told us where to find the cup," my father said.

"Did I? I really don't remember," she said. "Why do I feel cold and damp?"

"The result of your trance, I suppose. Come and sit by the fire in the hall."

Father led the way along the landing and down the main stairway into the entrance hall, then through the door into the main hall. Mother had the hornbook on her lap again. She hid it quickly under her embroidery as Father walked in. Meg jumped to her feet, looking guilty, and began sweeping the cinders that had fallen on the hearth.

"How was your meeting with Mistress Frith?" Mother asked.

"Very satisfactory," Father said. He turned to Meg. "Leave that hearth. Get out of here and work somewhere else."

Meg glared at him and pressed her lips tight to hold in the reply she really wanted to give. She bobbed a curtsey and hurried out of the hall.

Father turned back to Mother and said, "I am hoping I can lay my hands on the cup later today."

"That is remarkable," my mother said.

"Now, Mistress Frith," my father began.

"Call me Moll, please, Sir Jim."

"Moll. I want you to use your wonderful powers to tell me who the thieves are."

Moll took her pipe from her pocket and began to fill it from her tobacco pouch. She took a taper from the side of the hearth, lit it at the fire and began to suck the flame into the bowl of her pipe. All the time her eyes were darting round the room. "The thief. Yes."

"Who is it?"

"The cup isn't saying."

"I think it has something to do with Michael the Taverner," my father said.

Moll's reaction was startling. She choked for a few seconds, turned red in the face, and coughed out of control for a minute while Father slapped her on the back. Finally she cleared her throat and spat on the fire. "This smoke can sometimes catch you in the throat."

"Uncle George had the same problem when he smoked," my mother explained. "Now he just sucks on a cold pipe."

"I'll have to try it some time," said Moll. "What were you saying, Sir Jim?"

"Michael the Taverner was in the grounds when the cup went missing. I think he had something to do with it."

"No! No! I came from his place this morning and I didn't sense silver robbery coming from the Black Bull," she said.

"So? Who should I be looking for?"

"All I can tell you is you should look for a woman."

"I thought so."

"And this woman is closer than you think."

"I knew it!" Father crowed. He rubbed his hands. "You have confirmed my own suspicions! You have wonderful powers. I hope you will be able to help me with other cases in the future."

"I may not be staying in the district that long," said Moll.

"Why not?"

"Well, to be honest, Sir Jim – and no offence meant – but I find quiet little places like Marsden about as lively as a drainage ditch. There's not a lot happening here, is there?"

My father made an attempt at a smile. "Tomorrow you may see all the entertainment you want, Moll."

"Yes," Mother put in. "Tomorrow is Shrove Tuesday and we have a yearly football game. Marsden Village play against Birtley Village. It can be very exciting."

"I didn't mean the football, Marion," my father said. "I meant that tomorrow morning I am planning to hold a trial. In the afternoon you may have better sport when you see a thief executed."

"You've caught a thief?"

"First I will recover the cup, then I will charge the thief," he said.

"You know who it is?"

"But you told me yourself, Moll. It is a girl not so very far away from me."

Moll went very quiet for a few moments, then said, "I am a girl not very far away from you, Sir Jim."

My father's face creased again into that half-smile. "But a girl with your talents doesn't need to thieve for a living. A girl like you would never stoop so low as to steal a silver cup."

Moll brought her face close to my father's. His nose twitched with disgust as she breathed tobacco-breath in his face. "It's good to know you think like that, Sir Jim. Very good."

Moll nodded farewell to my mother and me and strode out of the door. Father looked after her fondly. "A clever girl, but she is wrong. She is too trusting. Michael Taverner gives her shelter and she only sees kindness in him. I'm the same myself – I see the best in people. But my nose tells me Michael Taverner is in this plot with our serving girl." He tapped the side of his nose in case we weren't sure where his nose was. "Tomorrow I want to see them swing side by side from the gallows. That will be greater sport than any football match."

CHAPTER NINE

"O barbarous and bloody spectacle!"

"Meg's still in danger," I said. "We ought to tell her."

"Perhaps not," my mother said.

We walked to the window and looked across the grass. A robin and two fieldfares chased one another as they fought over scraps of grain on the frozen ground. "Meg feeds them," my mother said.

"I know."

"We have to try to save her," she went on. "But there's no need to worry her. I'm sure Michael the Taverner is at the heart of all the trouble we've had."

"He and Wat Grey seem to be making a lot of money out of Moll Frith's soothsaying skills," I said.

"I'm sure they know the thief."

"You mean they steal the thief? Then why don't they sell the stolen goods? Why put it where Moll's powers can find it and let the owners have it back?" I asked.

"I don't know," said my mother. "I don't know about such things. We need to hear more."

"More about Michael and the goings-on in the Black Bull?"

My mother thought about it. The midday sun was bright and caught a flash of pink and blue as a jay swooped down to snatch up some food from the grass. "Yes," she said finally. "Perhaps your father's idea of a spy in the tavern was not such a bad one after all."

"But Meg is afraid that she'll find the thief and he will hang," I said.

"But you're not afraid of that, are you?"

"I don't want to be the cause of anyone's death," I said slowly, "but if they are guilty it's better they hang than Meg."

"Exactly," my mother agreed.

"So, if there's any more spying to be done, then I have to do it myself."

"It would be dangerous."

"I wouldn't mind that if I thought I was doing it for Meg," I said. "And, of course, I have a mother who's an expert spy!"

"I learned a lot when I was at Tutbury," she said. "Look, it's bright outside now. We'll put on our cloaks and ride over to Chester-le-Street market. There's something I'd like to buy and if I'm going to talk about my days in prison, I'll feel better in the open air."

My mother's cloak was a heavy dark-red wool. Today in the bright sunshine she wore the hood down. Grandfather was in the stable yard talking to Martin the

Ostler as he prepared our horses. The old man's pinched face peered up, framed by the thick fur collar. "There have been two attacks by a footpad in Bournmoor Woods in the past week," he warned us. "Constable Smith and some men from the village have searched through the trees and found nothing."

I laughed. "Father stopped them going too far. He said they'd disturb the deer."

"Deer! It'll cost him *dear* if your mother is the next victim," the old man snapped.

"They were farmers on foot who were attacked," my mother reminded him. "They don't seem brave enough to attack riders. And I have Will to protect me."

"He's a good lad," Grandfather agreed. My father had never called me "good". I wondered what I'd have to do to win his praise.

I mounted my roan mare and she danced on the spot. Since the frosts had come she hadn't had enough exercise. I made sure my sword wasn't covered by my cloak and I was ready to draw it at the first sign of trouble. Bournmoor Woods ought to be safe enough in the noonday sun. It was when we were returning at dusk that the footpads would be hidden in the shadows and looking for farmers with empty carts and full purses.

The path was wide enough for us to ride side by side. By the time we had reached Chester-le-Street market my mother had told me the story of her arrival at the dreadful castle at Tutbury.

This is her story in her own words, as best I can remember it ...

LADY MARSDEN'S STORY

Sir Amyas Paulet, the governor of the castle, took me into the deep window seat of his tower room. "No secret panels here," he said. "No tapestries for Queen Mary's spies to hide behind. I can speak to you freely now. In future I will treat you with the contempt the Queen and her friends would expect from me. If I give one small sign that you are sent by Walsingham, your life will be in danger. Poison is a favourite weapon of the Queen's."

"Surely she wouldn't kill me!" I said.

Paulet dragged down his mouth in a show of disgust. "Do not be fooled by the Queen. She can be fiery and proud, she can be tearful and sad. But whatever she seems, you have to remember that deep inside she is a ruthless woman. She wants power, and she does not care that innocent people like you and me have to die so she can get it."

I think I must still have looked disbelieving. Remember, I'd led a sheltered life and had heard of wicked men, but never wicked women. And Queen Mary was the hope of all good English Catholics. I had never heard stories of her cruel past. But Sir Amyas Paulet told them to me.

"Once upon a time there was a sad lady who was locked in a tower by a jealous queen. Along came a knight in shining armour. He slew the wicked queen and set the sad lady free from her tower. You've heard stories like that?"

I nodded.

"Well, the truth is, young Marion, there are hundreds of foolish young men who want to be knights in shining armour. But in this real world there is only one sad lady locked in a tower for them to rescue. Her name is Mary Queen of Scots. Queen Mary isn't the sweet sad lady you hear about in your old legends, but that doesn't matter. The foolish young men just *imagine* she is a helpless victim and Elizabeth is the wicked queen. There are lots of

people out there who want to free her. It is our job to stop them. Understand?"

"Yes, sir."

"Don't be fooled for one minute."

"No, sir."

"You have to remember that she was Queen of Scotland when she was just six days old. Her father was James V. He died of a broken heart when his armies were beaten at Solway Moss. What sort of man curls up and dies when his army is defeated? A weak man, young Marion – or a mad man. I sometimes think Queen Mary has some of her father's madness in her. There are times when she seems to want to give up the fight, turn her face to the wall and die just as her father did. At other times she rages against Queen Elizabeth and her prison guards and the whole world, screaming that she is a queen."

"She's a sad lady," I said.

Sir Amyas glared at me. "Have you listened to what I'm telling you, Marion? Have you? She is not a 'sad' lady. Sad ladies have bad luck heaped on their innocent heads, but Queen Mary brought all this on herself. She is a wil-ful woman. A spoilt child who has fits of sulks or fits of temper when the moods take her. And, just like a child, it's because she can't get her own way! Have you ever seen a child like that?"

"Yes, sir."

He sighed and looked across the bleak marshes, grey and dead even on a spring day. "I may seem hard on the woman, but you have to remember what she has done."

"Plotted against Queen Elizabeth?"

"No, I meant long before that. When she was fifteen she married the son of the French King, Dauphin Francis, but he died within two years and she lost that throne. So she came back to Scotland to rule. She was a Catholic queen in a Protestant country. The Scots forgave her that, but then she went and married her Catholic cousin, Henry Stuart, Lord Darnley. What would happen if our Queen Elizabeth had married a Catholic?"

"There'd have been a rebellion," I said.

"Exactly. And that's what happened in Scotland. The Protestants attacked with an army left by her half-brother and the Queen herself went out on to the battlefield."

"That was brave of her," I said.

The man shook his head. "What followed wasn't brave. It was cowardly. It was murder. Brave men and women fight on the battlefield – cowards murder their victims in their beds – or get someone else to do it for them. You see, Queen Mary started quarrelling with her husband, Darnley, within a year. He said he should get the throne if she died before him. His wife didn't agree. Darnley was as spoilt as she was. He thought her young secretary, David Riccio, was turning the Queen against him. So what did he do?"

"Arrested Riccio?" I asked.

"Nothing so polite as that. He wanted Riccio out of Queen Mary's way for good. Tell me, Marion, do you believe in soothsayers?"

"I don't know. I've never met one."

"There is a curious story that a soothsayer told Riccio to take the fortune he'd earned in Scotland and leave. Riccio laughed at the advice. He said, 'My enemies talk a lot, but they don't do a lot!' Ignoring the advice cost him his life."

"What happened?"

"One night in March, Queen Mary was having supper with Riccio and four friends. The young secretary was wearing his cap. That was something his enemies hated. Only a very special friend could wear a hat when he was in the presence of his queen. It was a small room, only twelve feet square, and most of the space was taken up by the dining table. It must have been hot because the room was warmed by a fire in a large hearth. Can you picture the scene, Marion?"

"I can."

"Not a scene of terror, you might think."

"No."

"In the middle of their meal, Queen Mary's husband, Darnley, arrived by a small back stairway from his own room below. He put his arm round the Queen – and that was a little unusual – they hadn't been too friendly lately. But still no one suspected what was to come. The Queen asked her husband if he had eaten and Darnley told her he had. Then they heard the sound of heavy footsteps and the rattle of armour coming up the main stairway. Imagine the shock when Darnley's friend, Lord Ruthven, stood there – there were stories that he was so ill he was close to death – and, stranger still, he was dressed in full armour, but had a nightgown over it."

"Was it a ghost?"

"No, it was not a ghost. Lord Ruthven spoke. He said he had come for David Riccio to punish him for his friendship with the Queen. Riccio ran round the table, clutched at Queen Mary's gown and tried to hide behind her. Darnley held the Queen tight while Ruthven's helpers rushed into the room. They bent Riccio's fingers back till he let go of the Queen's skirts. He was crying, 'Save me, lady, save me!' But she couldn't. Riccio was still trying to hide behind the Queen. One of the killers struck at him over the Queen's shoulder. She said later that she had felt the cold steel rush past her neck."

"Did they hurt her?"

"One of the killers held a pistol to her side, she says, and pulled the trigger. The gun misfired, but she was sure they planned to kill her too."

"But they killed her secretary, Riccio?"

"They butchered him. His body was found with fifty-six wounds in it. Fifty-six! Darnley didn't just want Riccio dead – he wanted the man killed in the most brutal way while his queen watched. Then the Scottish lords made her their prisoner. Of course she escaped. Mary Queen of Scots is an expert at escaping. That's why we have to be so careful. And her favourite method is to get the help of men. She charms them and they help her to escape."

"So who helped her escape that time?" I asked.

"Believe it or not, it was Darnley himself. She told him she would forgive him if he helped her escape, and he believed her. A few nights later, while the other killers watched the tower where she slept, she slipped through a back entrance and crossed a graveyard. She must have gone right past Riccio's new grave. What sort of woman can do that?" Sir Amyas asked me.

"A courageous woman," I replied. "But I thought you said *she* was the murderer?"

"I'm coming to that. The Queen wanted to divorce Darnley after he had Riccio killed."

"You can't blame her for that," I murmured. Sir Amyas leaned forward, his eyes opening wide with the horror of his story.

"But when Darnley refused she had another plan. Darnley had been ill and was living in a house to the south of Edinburgh. The house was right up against the town wall. Deep in the night he was asleep in his bed behind curtains of royal purple. His servant, William Taylor, slept in a pallet bed at his side, and another servant, Thomas Nelson, slept outside in the gallery. Darnley was disturbed by noises outside his window. He dragged himself to the window and looked out. Some men were gathering below his window. He suspected that they might be going to set fire to the house. With Taylor's help he climbed out of the window and down the wall."

"How could he do that if he was so ill?" I asked.

"Some say Taylor made a rope of sheets and lowered Darnley down in a chair. But it did him no good. The house was surrounded. Men began to close in on him from the shadows. A woman in a nearby house heard him cry out, 'Have pity on me for the love of Jesus who had mercy on all the world!' They were his last words. Some say he was strangled with the sleeves of his own shirt and others that he was smothered with his velvet and fur nightgown. Taylor died too. The killers made sure there were no marks on the bodies because they wanted to make the murder look like an accident."

"They set fire to the house?" I guessed.

"No. The cellars were filled with gunpowder, and they lit the fuse and rode off. They scarcely got away before the house exploded with the force of thirty cannon. The whole of Edinburgh was woken by the blast. Many rushed to the garden and saw the bodies of Darnley and his servant. But everyone agreed that they hadn't died in the blast – the house was ruined, but the corpses weren't

even singed. Somehow Thomas Nelson survived to tell the tale of Darnley's last hours."

Sir Amyas Paulet looked at me. "What sort of woman could pretend to forgive her husband, then take such a terrible revenge?" he asked me.

I shivered. This was the woman I was going to spy upon. If she ever suspected me of betraying her, who knows how she'd act? It seemed certain that she would find some way of avenging herself. "Maybe she wasn't the one who planned her husband's murder," I objected weakly. "After all, he must have had other enemies."

"The Queen had been with Darnley in the house, but she had gone to a wedding and was spending the night there because it was too far to travel home. Isn't it strange that she was away on the very night of the explosion?"

"It might have been a plot to kill her as well," I suggested.

Sir Amyas shook his head. "There was one man who was suspected of leading the plot to murder Darnley: James Hepburn, the Earl of Bothwell. Barely three months later Mary Queen of Scots had married the earl, the man who almost certainly killed her husband."

I had to admit that Queen Mary seemed to be guilty of this terrible crime. "If that's true it is shocking," I said.

"It was so shocking that the nobles of Scotland turned against her. She raised an army to fight them, but they defeated her. She was imprisoned at Lochleven and her baby son was crowned King James VI. She escaped from Lochleven, even though it's on an island. Remember this, Marion," Sir Amyas said fiercely, "she escapes. Always escapes! But she won't escape from me." He gave a grim smile and he slapped the cold stone of the walls. Thick walls that would hold an army out – or a queen in.

"Of course, when she fled from Scotland she turned to her cousin Queen Elizabeth for shelter," Sir Amyas went on. "Elizabeth has had her locked away ever since. It's curious that this prison is the one she walked into herself."

"What will my duties be?" I asked.

"You will have duties to Queen Mary – you'll do whatever she asks. But your first duty will be to me and your real queen, Elizabeth. You will report everything that Queen Mary says or does that will put England at risk. Everything." The governor paced across the cold room. "Our England is too small for two queens, Marion. I have a feeling that one of them will have to die soon." He looked at me with eyes as grey and hard as the stone of his castle. "You must make sure that Queen Mary is the one to die."

CHAPTER TEN

"Be poisonous too and kill thy forlorn queen"

My mother finished the story of her arrival at Tutbury as we rode into Chester-le-Street. Crowds of shouting, laughing, arguing, crying people milled through the market place. The greatest crush was round the stalls of salted fish as housewives tried to buy fish for the Lent season that started two days later.

We left the horses in the care of the stables at the Lambton Arms. The young ostler warned us, "Watch out for cutpurses, young sir. Two of my customers have lost their money already today."

I tucked my purse inside my doublet. "Two in one morning," my mother sighed. "Chester-le-Street market doesn't usually have two in a month. There's something happening in this area, Will. It's a wave of wickedness that your father can't control in spite of his brave words."

We walked down the High Street towards the open market at the bottom of the hill. The shutters of the shops were pulled down and spread with the shopkeepers' goods. Crowds of buyers blocked the narrow pavement and forced us to walk in the muddy road. We were jostled by horses and splashed by lumbering carts who didn't seem to think we had any right to be on their road.

Before we reached the market my mother took a turn up a narrow quiet alley between wood-framed houses. The upper storeys were built out over the footpath till they almost met the houses opposite. It made the alley gloomy and the air stagnant. Slops had been thrown from the upstairs windows and not enough rain could fall on to the pathway to wash it clean.

We picked our way between the piles of filth. "Why are we coming up this way?" I asked nervously. It was a good place for the cutthroats and thieves to hide and leap out on their victims. I rested my hand on my dagger, ready for trouble.

"Don't worry, Will," my mother smiled. "This is the poorest part of town. Thieves prefer the other end of the High Street where the rich traders are."

"So why are we here?"

"To see a dressmaker."

I sniffed. "She can't be very good if she lives in this sort of back lane."

"She is *too* good, Will. She takes so much care with each dress that she doesn't make enough to live on. I pay her what her dresses are really worth, but you know your father only allows me three new dresses a year. It's not enough to make her rich."

We came to a wooden door that was cracked and warped with age. Mother lifted the latch and stepped inside the gloomy hallway. She turned left into a room where a woman sat at the window sewing. Children played at her feet with some knucklebones from a sheep's foot. I'd played that game myself when I was younger, throwing the bones in the air and catching as many as possible on the back of my hand.

The woman had colourless hair and a thin, unhealthy face. She was about Mother's age, but her back was bent and her shoeless feet blue with the cold. "You should take more care of yourself, Elise," my mother sighed.

"I do my best, Lady Marsden," the woman said with a smile. "Are you ready for your new Easter dress already?" she asked. She had a strong French accent.

"This time it isn't for me," my mother explained. "It's for one of our serving girls."

"What material do you want?" the dressmaker asked.

"Nothing too fine. Sir James will be horrified when he finds I'm having a dress made. She usually wears cast-offs from the children of the other servants, but her black day dress is faded to grey and worn through in places. Her best church dress is probably older than I am."

"So you want wool?"

"Yes. But a fine wool."

The woman reached into a chest, almost the only piece of furniture in the room. She pulled out some scraps of material. "The draper in Pelton has these materials. Would you like to choose?"

My mother took the samples and studied each one carefully, feeling it gently then holding it up to the daylight. "This one. The green. It will go with her eyes," she said.

Elise nodded. "And the size?"

"She's a thin girl. She comes up to Will's shoulder."

"You want it for Easter?"

"No. I want it for tomorrow if possible. It's a celebration. I know it's not much time, but I'll pay double."

After paying the seamstress and arranging to have the dress delivered we stepped back into the alley and headed for the market again. "What are we celebrating?" I asked.

"Meg being cleared of the charge of stealing the silver cup."

"You think we can do it?" I asked.

"I am sure *you* can," my mother said.

We reached the main street and joined the crowds. We didn't need any of the market goods because Marsden Manor provided most of our food, and part of our lands included a stretch of the River Wear so we always had fish. Still, we enjoyed wandering round looking at the shops and stalls that sold everything from bread to buttons and magical charms to cheeses. We kept away from the pit at the far end of the market where cheering crowds were watching bull-baiting and cockfighting. My mother said it sickened her, although I'd like to have seen these shows just once.

I took notice of the beggars in a way I'd never done before. The way they moved, their voices and expressions. If I were going to play a dummerer again I wanted to do it properly.

By the time we had collected our horses from the Lambton Arms the heavy clouds were gathering from the north and darkening the alleyways to early dusk. "It'll be dark by the time we reach Bournmoor Woods," I said.

"Don't worry, Will. There'll be plenty of people travelling that road on their way home."

"I've heard of no one losing their purse this afternoon," the ostler said as he threw my mother's saddle over her horse.

"No," I said. "They seem to cut purses during the day, then go off to hide in the woods to catch the farmers travelling home in the afternoon."

"Cutpurses and footpads aren't the same thing at all, Will," my mother said as she guided her horse out of the stable yard and on to the crowded High Street. "And then there is the burglar who stole our cup."

"No, but there must be some link," I said.

A man in a mud-spattered jerkin stood in the roadway with a sheaf of papers in his hand. He was passing a printed sheet to everyone who rode by. "Beat the thieves, ladies and gentlemen! Beat the thieves!" he cried. When we reached him he thrust a sheet at us with a gap-toothed grin. "Had anything stolen, young sir?" he asked. "Get it back!"

I took the crudely printed handbill from him and read it aloud to my mother. "It's an advertisement for Moll Frith! It says she is at the Black Bull Tavern in Marsden Village every evening to help people find stolen goods. All she asks in return is a fair reward."

"At least this outburst has brought someone some good," said my mother.

"Only the way a dead dog might bring good to some maggots," I said.

As we rode clear of the towering houses the fresh northerly wind stung our faces. We were heading back to Marsden Hall, the house that one day I would own.

"When I was born, Marsden Manor had an heir," I said. "But you would have liked a daughter, wouldn't you?"

"You are a good son, Will. I am proud of you."

"You would like a daughter *as well*."

"A daughter would have been nice."

"And you are teaching Meg to read. You are buying her dresses. She is the daughter you haven't got?"

"So what if she is?"

"So – so it's more important than ever that we save her from the noose," I said grimly.

"You are a good son, Will. You understand a lot for a boy of your age."

"Tell me about Mary Queen of Scots and your spying," I said. "I need to get it right. We haven't much time. When you met the Queen, was she really as bad as Sir Amyas Paulet said?"

"No one is simply bad or good, Will. She was a mixture, the same as all of us."

"Great-Uncle George told me we're all a mixture of the four elements – air, earth, fire and water. Do you believe that?" I asked.

"If it's true, then Queen Mary was mostly fire. She had raging tempers. Yet she could be as cold as water. That's what made her so dangerous, I suppose. She was burning with fury when David Riccio was killed, but she hid it well. Her revenge against Darnley was as cold as iced water."

We crunched through the ice that was forming on the puddles in the road as my mother told her story.

◆ 94 ◆

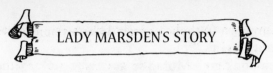

My duties were to help Mary Queen of Scots with her daily life: her dressing and washing and hairdressing and eating. After supper each evening another two ladies-in-waiting helped her with preparations for bed and slept in the room with her.

Sir Amyas Paulet led me to the Queen's chambers in the west tower of Tutbury Castle. That was where I first met my partner. "This is Morag MacNeil," Sir Amyas said. "For the past few months she's been Lady Mary's only daytime companion. She'll be glad of some help, won't you, Morag?"

The girl was my own age. She had black hair scraped back firmly into a blue bow on her neck. Her straight black eyebrows almost met in the middle and added to the fierce expression in her dark-brown eyes. She smiled politely and said, "Thank you, Sir Amyas," in a strong Scots accent.

Sir Amyas left us. He closed the door, but I heard no key in the lock. When I turned back to Morag, the smile had slipped from her face. She was glaring at me. "Are you one of his spies?" she asked.

"No, I'm not," I lied. I was shocked at how easily the lie slipped out.

"My poor lady is surrounded by enemies, but the ones she really hates are the ones who pretend to be friends, then betray her."

"I am here to serve her," I said.

"If you do betray her I'll cut your throat myself," Morag said.

I was shaken. Maybe that was what she wanted. Maybe this was a test. I decided the best response was anger. "I want to see a Catholic queen on the throne of England. I'm sick of Elizabeth and her persecution. I want to worship in my own Catholic church. I don't want to go to her Protestant services."

"Then don't go," Morag spat.

"The government has raised the fine to twenty pounds a month for Catholics who miss the services. My family would be ruined in a year if we all refused. I have to go. That's why I'm here. At least I can worship with my fellow Catholics, can't I?"

Morag seemed to relax. "That's why I'm here too. How can the Protestants keep my poor lady trapped in here like an animal?" she asked. "She's so good and kind. I'm sure jailer Paulet told you tales of my lady's past, did he?"

"He did."

"They are Protestant lies," Morag said.

"I'm pleased to hear it. I wouldn't want to serve a lady who had done the things Sir Amyas said."

Morag looked away from me for a few moments. "That's not to say she's an easy lady to work for. She suffers."

"Suffers?"

"Her health. She has good days and bad days. Today's a bad day." She looked me in the eyes again. "But don't judge her on what you see today. She may say harsh things to you, but she'll regret it tomorrow. You have to forgive her. She is suffering a lot. Never forget that."

The small room we were in had a door to the outside and another door that I guessed led into the tower. From behind that massive oak door came a voice with a Scots accent. It had all the force that a queen could command: "Morag! Morag! Where are you?"

Morag opened the door to the inner room, entered and dropped a deep curtsey. "Your Majesty, it's your new lady-in-waiting, Marion Ashton."

I followed Morag into the room. Before looking up I curtseyed even lower than Morag and stayed down. "Get up, child," the Queen ordered.

I rose and looked at the woman sitting on a chair at the window. Her body was slightly hunched as if she were in pain. Her fine face was lined. But it was her eyes that shocked me. Wild, dangerous eyes like those of a half-crazed horse my brother had once tried to ride. It had thrown him and broken his arm. I wondered what hurt my journey with Mary Queen of Scots would bring me.

"Come closer, Marion, and let me look at you," the Queen said. "It's a good name, Marion. It's another way of saying Mary, you know. And Morag here is a Scottish way of saying Mary. And I have a Maria as a night maid. Did you know that? Now we are four Maries!"

"Yes, madam," I said as I slowly came closer to her. "What are my duties?"

"Oh, Marion, my child. Surely you know *that*! Morag here will take care of my wigs and clothes and food. You have been sent here with just one duty. Just one! To help me escape, isn't that right?"

"Yes, madam," I said. I didn't dare meet the wild eyes.

"There have been other attempts, you know."

"I know nothing about them."

"Always betrayed by men," she hissed. "I haven't always been held in a fortress like this. I was at Chatsworth sixteen years ago. A group of local squires were going to carry me off to the Isle of Man when I went out riding, but one of them betrayed the plot. I should have learned never to trust men. But you're a woman, Marion. With your help I'll be free and claim my thrones."

"We will need the help of *some* men," I said carefully.

"Which men?"

"Gilbert Gifford, who is carrying our messages to France," I reminded her.

"I have always wondered if he is loyal."

"Gifford is every bit as loyal as I am," I said. For once I was telling the truth!

"Then we trust Gifford," she said. "And Morag here."

The girl looked across at me coldly. I thought that the Queen was offering me too much of her confidence too soon and Morag was jealous.

"Now, Marion, I have trusted too many men. There was a plot by an Italian called Ridolphi. An army from Spain was to invade and set me on the throne of England. I would marry the Duke of Norfolk and we'd become King and Queen of England."

"What went wrong?"

"My letters to Ridolphi were discovered. That won't happen this time. Your friend Gifford and I have a secret code. If the letters ever fall into the wrong hands, no one will understand them."

"I see."

"I will teach you the code, Marion. You will write my letters for me."

"Yes, madam."

"Morag here will do all the work I need in these apartments. She can cook and clean for you too. But she's no use when it comes to writing letters. She can barely read."

Morag's face was blank, but I knew she must hate me for my cleverness. And she had suddenly been made my servant.

◆ 98 ◆

"What happened to Ridolphi's plot?" I asked.

"One of our messengers, Charles Bailly, was arrested and some letters found. My cousin Elizabeth had some of my closest advisers tortured and they told her all they knew. She never trusted me again after that. Her parliament turned against me. One of her ministers called me a 'monstrous dragon' and Elizabeth allowed it! Poor Norfolk was executed at the Tower of London, but Elizabeth didn't dare to execute me. Do you know why not?"

"No, madam."

"Because I am a rightful queen of royal blood, just as she is. If killing me is lawful, then killing her would be lawful. I am safe. Elizabeth will never execute me."

"I see."

"Yes, Marion. I think you do. You are a clever girl. It has taken me eighteen years to learn all I need to know, eighteen years in miserable places like this. But now I have the secrets I need to unlock my prison. Trust no man unless you have to, Marion, and make sure all our letters are in code."

"Yes, madam."

"And there is one more thing I have learned if my escape is to be successful."

"What is that, madam?"

"Not to be too tenderhearted. In the past I have made plans to escape and take Elizabeth's crown. Next time it won't be that way at all. Next time something has to happen before I set foot out of my prison."

"What is that, madam?"

The Queen of Scots' eyes glowed in the dim light of her room. "Next time I am going to arrange to have Queen Elizabeth assassinated first!"

CHAPTER ELEVEN

"I hope you'll come to supper"

By the time my mother had reached that point in her story we were entering Bournmoor Woods. It was sheltered amongst the bare trees, although the top boughs swayed and groaned in the wind.

"You see the problem of being a spy, Will? You think your job is just to sit there and watch. But it won't be that simple. Sooner or later you have to make a decision about whose side you are on."

"And whose side were *you* on, back in Tutbury?" I asked.

"I thought I was a Catholic, forced to spy on a good queen to help destroy her. I found I was spying on a dangerous woman who was planning murder."

"What has that to do with my spying in the Black Bull tonight?" I asked.

"Maybe nothing," she answered. "But suppose we are wrong, as I was wrong when I went to Tutbury. Suppose you find that Meg really is a thief?"

"She isn't!" I cried. "We know she isn't!"

"That's what we want to believe, Will – just as I wanted to believe Queen Mary was an innocent and unhappy queen. Whose side was I on in Tutbury? Oh, Will, if only it was that simple. Ask yourself – if you find Meg is guilty of theft, whose side will you be on tomorrow?"

I was saved from having to answer by a noise that came

from our right. We were at the place where the road from Chester-le-Street is joined by the road from the river bank. A gure staggered from the side road and into our path. In the near darkness I could make out that it was a thin man with a beard. I couldn't see his face. He was groaning, "Help me! Help me! I've been robbed."

At once I sensed a terrible danger. I grabbed the bridle of my mother's horse and called, "Ride for your life, Mother!"

"Let go of my horse, Will," she said calmly.

I released her bridle, drew my sword and kicked my horse forward so it stood between her and the strange man. "It's an old trick!" I shouted to her. "You stop to help the man, then his footpad friends jump out of the undergrowth and rob you."

"Will!" she said in a level voice, but with the first hint of anger I had ever heard in it. "If you don't get down and help him then I shall!"

"That's what they want! They want us to get down off our horses! It's a trap!"

"Help me! I've been beaten!" the man wailed.

"Get down at once, Will!" Mother said, her voice as

sharp as my sword. "You cannot leave your own father to stumble round in the woods like this."

"What?"

"I said, help your father. Get him up on your horse if you can and lead him back to Marsden Hall."

"My father?"

"Of course it's your father. Now, for pity's sake, help him."

I peered forward into the gloom. The man raised his face towards us and the last of the weak daylight showed me she was right.

I jumped to the ground and, keeping my sword in one hand, helped my father into my saddle. "Are you all right, Father?"

"All right, he asks! All right? What sort of imbecile question is that, you lobcock?"

"James," my mother said, "Will is trying to help. Just tell us what happened."

"Can I not at least get back to Marsden Hall before I bleed to death?" he asked. But then, back at the hall, he fell silent and refused to answer any more questions.

The ostler took our horses and I put Father's arm round my shoulder and helped him into the hall. Grandmother was playing chess by the fireside as we staggered into the large room. "Really, Will, you are getting too softhearted, bringing beggars into the hall. Couldn't you just leave him to be fed in the kitchen?"

"It's me!" my father cried. "See! I'm so badly battered even my own mother doesn't recognize me!"

"Oh, sit down and stop fussing," Grandmother said. "That was a little jest, son. You never were very good at understanding jests, were you?"

"What happened?" I asked.

"I was coming up the path from the river when I was attacked!"

"Start at the beginning, my boy," Grandfather said. "What were you doing down by the river? Fishing? Swimming?"

"I went down there to find the missing silver cup," Father told him. Mother was dabbing at the blood on his face with a cloth and water warmed in a pan over the fire. She sprinkled a few herbs into the water. Their smell was sweet and soothing. "I had information that the cup may have been placed in the water where the thief could recover it later. I decided I'd get there first."

Grandfather leaned back in his seat at the fireplace and folded his hands in his lap. "If it had been me, I would have arranged for the constable and a few strong men to hide by the river and watch to see who came to recover the cup. That way you'd have found out who the thief is."

My father glared at him. "Except, in this case, I already *know* who the thief is. It's that miserable little serving girl. She'll hang for it tomorrow."

Grandmother looked at him sharply. "I hope you have a good reason for saying that, James. Lord Lambton doesn't like magistrates who hang suspects up like sides of bacon in the pantry. Last year our friend Birtley didn't hang a single person."

"So everyone keeps telling me," Father snapped. "But a footpad who attacks a magistrate and steals his silver cup is bound to hang!"

"Are you saying young Meg is a footpad?" Grandfather asked.

"Of course not!"

"Then who robbed you?"

"A huge brute of a man. His shoulders were as wide as that doorway. I'd been fishing in the water under the bridge for half an hour before I finally found the cup. I'll swear my hand had icicles hanging from it. When I turned to walk back home, he was standing there. 'Give me the cup!' he cried. 'I'll die first!' I told him. Then we struggled, but it was icy and I slipped. Otherwise he'd never have overcome me."

"What was this footpad armed with?" asked Grandfather.

"A club. A wooden club, cut from a tree – and as heavy as this table."

Grandmother rose stiffly and walked over to him. She placed her hands on Father's head and felt it. "He didn't break your skull, son. In fact I can't feel any lumps even."

"He didn't actually hit me."

She looked at his face that had been cleaned by Mother. "There are just scratches from brambles."

"They were the sharpest thorn bushes you ever saw!" Father grumbled.

Grandmother nodded. "So, James. A fellow waved the branch of a tree at you. You dropped the cup and ran off into the bushes. Is that it?"

"He was bigger than me, Mother," my father said, dabbing at the scratches on his face.

"That's not much of a description to give the constable," Grandfather said. "A lot of people are bigger than you. What was he wearing?"

"It was dark."

"Think, James. I realize you were terrified …"

"I was *not* terrified. I was about to defend myself, but I slipped."

"Very well," Grandfather sighed. "But, before you slipped, you must have noticed something that will help the constable. Was he wearing a hat?"

"A cap – pulled down over his ears."

"Could you see his hair?"

"It was fair."

"And his face?"

"He had a handkerchief over the bottom half of his face and a cloak over his clothes."

Father was interrupted by a rap on the door. It swung open and Moll Frith ambled in. "Nobody in the kitchen," she said. "Just let myself in. Hope you don't mind, Sir Jim! Hey! You been in a fight with a cat, have you?"

"No," he said shortly. "What can I do for you?"

"I just wondered if you'd found your cup. 'Cos, if you have, you can give me my ten shillings reward!" she said with a wide grin.

Father glared at her for a minute. "I do not have the cup," he said finally.

"Really? I'd have sworn it was in a river under a bridge."

"I thought you were in a trance when you said that!" I said. "I thought you couldn't remember what you said?"

"Yes, young Will, but your father reminded me what I'd said when I came out of my trance. But I'm disappointed," she went on, turning back to Father. "Did you look where I told you?"

"Yes."

"And no cup there!"

"I didn't say that."

"So there was a cup there?"

"Yes."

"The one that you lost?"

"Yes."

"Then you owe me ten shillings!"

"But I haven't got the cup. No sooner had I found it than it was stolen from me," my father cried.

"Sorry about that, Sir Jim. But that's not my fault. You said you'd pay me to find it. I found it – so you pay me."

"That's not fair!" he wailed.

Moll looked round at the family. Everyone was listening

with interest. "What do you good folk reckon?"

Grandfather cleared his throat. "I have served my time as a magistrate. I think there was clearly a contract between you two. You, Moll Frith, have kept your part of the contract. I'm afraid my son must pay up."

My father gave Grandfather a spiteful look, put his hand into his purse and pulled out some silver shillings. "I only have eight," he said.

"That's all right, Sir Jim. I'll collect the rest later."

"It's all you're getting," he said.

Moll clicked her fingers. "Tell you what, Sir Jim! Let's play for double or nothing, shall we?"

"What do you mean?"

"I mean, I'll try again to find your cup. If you get it back and keep it, you pay me ten shillings plus the two you still owe me for finding it first time. If you don't get it back, then I'll let you off the two shillings you owe me. That sounds fair to me, Sir Jim." She turned to Grandfather. "What do you think, sir?"

"I think you're an impudent witch," said Grandfather.

"But a good one," Moll grinned. She stretched out her hand towards Father, "Do you agree?"

Father slapped her hand, then wiped his own hand on the side of his black gown. "I agree. Now tell me where the cup is this time."

"Sorry, Sir Jim. I have to get down to the Black Bull and have a bit to eat before my customers start arriving tonight. Come along to the tavern and I'll see what I can do for you."

"I am not setting foot in that filthy den."

"Why not? Michael the Taverner comes here, doesn't he?"

"I don't like the idea of a magistrate being seen in a common public house like that."

"You don't want your cup back, then?"

Father strode to the door. He clutched at the doorpost and said, "I don't feel too well after that attack, Marion. Have my supper sent up to my room. I'm going to bed."

"So you're not going to the Black Bull to find out about your cup?"

"I would do if I were well enough. I suppose you'll just have to do it for me, Marion. I'm not well. Not well at all."

"Very good, dear," Mother nodded as he marched off down the hall and up the stairway.

Moll's moon-face gazed round at us happily. "Of course the food in the tavern is awful stuff. Boiled meat and vegetables every night. I'll bet you're having something tasty for supper tonight."

"Roast goose, beef pasties and pears in syrup," my mother said.

"No fish?" Moll said. "I like a nice bit of fish."

"After tomorrow we'll be eating fish all through Lent so I'll spare the family that tonight," Mother smiled.

"Still, that goose sounds very tasty. Sounds more like the stuff I'm used to in London. Pity you don't have a few scraps to spare for Moll Frith, isn't it?"

"Yes," Grandfather said sourly. "It is a great pity. We would love to have had your company."

"I wouldn't swear or spit on your new carpet," she said. "I learned good manners from some of the rich folk I've worked for."

"You were a servant?" Grandfather asked.

"No! I was an entertainer. I can juggle and dance. I worked for a touring theatre company and I can do magic. Of course, you know about my fortune-telling, but I'm also a great singer."

The truth was she sang like a crow, but I could see Grandfather was amused as well as disgusted by Moll.

"On behalf of the Marsden family I'd like to invite you to eat with us," he said suddenly. "We don't have many guests – James does not usually like strangers in the house. But he'll be out of the way. You are welcome to stay, Moll."

Grandmother looked startled, but all she said was, "You can wash in the kitchen."

"What for?"

"Why – why – because your hands are dirty!" Grandmother said. It was true that the palms and fingers of Moll's hands were stained brown.

"I don't eat with my hands, you know!" Moll said. "I learned my manners in some of the finest houses in the country. I eat with my knife and spoon. Why, I've even eaten with those new spears from Italy."

"They're called forks," Mother nodded.

"See!" Moll cried. "I bet you've eaten with lords and ladies all your life."

Grandmother leaned forward and waved a clawed finger at the yellow-haired woman. "Lady Marsden has eaten with a queen!"

"She's never!"

"She has indeed! Lady Marsden was a lady-in-waiting to Mary Queen of Scots!"

"I've heard about her! Our Queen Bess gave her a hair cut when I was a babe. And you worked for her, Marion, did you?"

"I did," my mother admitted.

"Tell me what she was like."

My mother collected the bowl of herbs and the cloth she'd used to wash my father's scratches. "I have to arrange dinner now, Moll. But we have a custom in this house. After dinner someone usually tells the family a story. If the rest of the family don't mind, I could tell you about Mary Queen of Scots."

"Did you know my real name is Mary?"

"Moll is usually a pet name for Mary," my mother nodded.

"And I'm just like her. Brave and beautiful!"

There was a silence in the room as my family tried to take in this comparison. Finally Grandfather said, "Yes, Moll. But, when *you're* in trouble, I'll bet you never lose your head!"

First Moll chuckled, then she laughed. By the time she reached the kitchen to wash she was roaring. The sound rang down the hollow corridors of the ancient house.

CHAPTER TWELVE

"Here's a pot of good double beer"

Dinner was a happy event that evening. Without Father's damp spirit hovering over the dinner table we laughed a lot. Talk at dinner was usually quiet and about the business of the manor. But whoever had taught Moll her manners had forgotten to tell her that ladies spoke *quietly* at the dinner table.

Grandfather carved large slices of goose for her and Great-Uncle George kept her wine cup full. Having her mouth full didn't stop her talking and goose grease was sprayed in all directions. No one seemed to notice or mind very much. Grandmother didn't mind Moll's coarse language, Grandfather wasn't shocked by her disgraceful stories and Great-Uncle George wasn't upset that he couldn't talk as much as usual.

I was thrilled to hear her tales of the theatre in London. To act on the London stage was my dream.

Mother listened wide-eyed and wondering. We were all happy.

Meg brought extra pears in syrup from the kitchens when Moll ate all the fruit from the bowl on the table. No one had the heart to tell her it was intended to serve the whole family.

Then Meg sat at Mother's feet as we all moved away from the table to sit by the fire. Grandfather, Grandmother, Great-Uncle George and I sat round a low table to play a game of cards while Mother and Moll sat at opposite sides of the hearth to talk.

My mind wasn't on the game of cards and I lost most hands. I was listening to my mother's story ...

LADY MARSDEN'S STORY

When I knew Mary Queen of Scots she was a prisoner. A *real* prisoner.

It hadn't always been that way. When Queen Elizabeth first held her, she lived like a queen in a palace. She had thirty people to make her life as comfortable as possible – her own secretary and her own cooks. Even some of her servants had servants.

Queen Mary was always sickly, but as long as she was allowed to ride out and get fresh air she was well enough. But when Queen Elizabeth decided that Queen Mary was getting too much pleasure from her imprisonment, life became harder. The more she was kept in stinking castles like Tutbury the worse her health became. The poor lady had a constant pain in her side that stopped her sleeping. She had weeks of sickness and, when I knew her, her legs were so painful that she always walked with a limp.

One of my main duties was to write Queen Mary's letters for her when the pain in her arm made it too difficult. In every letter to her friends and supporters she complained about her health. She also complained about her jailer, Sir Amyas Paulet. He didn't seem to believe she was really ill. He thought she was just deceiving everyone into thinking she was a weak and sickly woman. He was sure that if she got free she would be strong enough to rule the kingdom.

"Paulet is an animal," she would say on the days when she was strong. "I once gave an old dress to a poor beggar woman out of pity. He said I was only trying to win the hearts of the English people! He used that as an excuse to stop me riding out of the castle. But I tell you, Marion, when I am queen Sir Amyas Paulet will be the first to die."

On the days when she was weak and ill she would moan, "I will die in prison, Marion. The letters from France have stopped. Even my friends over the sea have forgotten me. That's what my cousin Elizabeth is hoping for. That's why she orders Paulet to treat me so cruelly." Then she would sit and weep silently for hour after hour. Her favourite dog played at her feet, jumped up and licked her hand, but she took no notice of it.

After a month or so the captivity started to make me as gloomy as the Queen. It was true that Gilbert Gifford's letters had not been delivered in their secret beer barrels for weeks. With no news coming from outside it made us all feel cut off.

Sir Amyas Paulet made it worse when he stopped us from walking on the battlements of the castle. "You could wave to passersby," he said, "and the waves could be signals. If you want to walk in the fresh air, then you do it in the castle courtyard and not on the walls."

Every day the foul smell of the castle grew stronger, Queen Mary grew weaker and I grew more desperate. At last Sir Amyas could see that Queen Mary really was a very sick woman. He looked down on her as she lay moaning in her bed and said, "It's the air from the sewers. The drains are blocked with human waste. The whole castle needs to be abandoned while they're cleaned out."

"We're leaving Tutbury?" I said.

"Sir Francis Walsingham says we can move to the castle

at Chartley," he said. "Begin to pack your lady's belongings. We leave tomorrow."

"She's too ill to travel," Morag said fiercely. "She'll die."

"I thought your queen said she would die if she stayed here. Which is it to be?"

Morag glared at him and bent over her mistress to explain what was happening. Queen Mary spoke in a whisper. Morag looked up. "We'll go to Chartley," she said.

The journey almost did kill the Queen. She lay sick for four weeks in her new prison. Then one day I was sent to the gatehouse to direct the unloading of some fresh beer for the Queen. The man in a leather apron and wide-brimmed hat grunted, "Special delivery for the Queen."

The barrel was too heavy for me. "I can't carry that," I said.

"Then I'll have to carry it for you," he said, throwing it over his shoulder. His face was hidden from me by the barrel. I led the way to the Queen's apartments, past the guards and into her kitchens. The man in the apron put the barrel carefully on the floor while one of Sir Amyas Paulet's guards watched. He looked up and under the cover of the hat brim he winked at me. I saw the face of Gilbert Gifford for a brief moment. Then he was gone.

The guard tapped at the barrel and heard the dull sound of a full container. If he had tapped the lid, he might have heard the hollow sound of the secret compartment that held the letters. I drew off some of the beer and handed it to him. He drank it and licked his lips. "Better stuff than we get," he grumbled.

"Fit for a queen," I said, trying to hide the excitement in my voice.

"A traitor more like," the man said, and went back to his duty on patrol. I took one of the kitchen knives and scooped out some of the wax that held the secret panel in place. I lifted the flap of wood, pushed my hand inside and pulled out a packet of letters wrapped in oiled cloth to protect them.

I hid the letters under my gown and hurried up the winding stone stairway to the Queen's room. Morag was sewing by the window while the Queen sat up in bed brushing her thin greying hair. They seemed to sense my excitement as soon as I entered the room. "What is it, Marion?" Morag asked.

"Letters!" I said. "Letters from Gilbert Gifford's beer barrel!"

The Queen's pale, thin hands flew together in prayer. After a minute she opened her eyes and said, "Read them, Marion."

I opened the packet and took out the letters. Some were in French, from the Queen's supporters in Spain and France. But one was in Queen Mary's own secret code. "Should I decode this one, madam?" I asked.

"Yes, Marion."

I took out a wax tablet from the desk and sat next to Morag on the window seat. We always used a wooden tray filled with hard wax to write down the decoded messages so that we could scrape them off as soon as we knew what they said. The Queen was impatient and livelier than I had seen her since we arrived at Chartley. "What does it say?" she asked every five minutes.

It must have been an hour before I was able to report to my mistress. In that time Morag had helped her to dress and had put a fine dark-brown wig on the Queen's head.

"The letter talks of a time when your jailer was the Earl of Shrewsbury," I said.

"A fine man, even if he is an English Protestant. He treated me like a queen. For a long time his wife Bess was my closest companion. Is he to take over from the loathsome Paulet?"

"No, madam. The letter speaks of a page that he had. A youngster called Anthony Babington who became devoted to you when he was in the service of the Earl of Shrewsbury," I explained.

"What about him?"

"He is now a man of twenty-five."

"What is this to do with me?" The Queen gave a heartfelt sigh. "I was beautiful then. I was as thin as a willow and my skin was as fine as yours, Marion."

"You're still beautiful," Morag said quickly.

"Thank you, child. I still hope that some man will find me attractive when I am free of this place."

"They will," Morag promised. "They all will."

The Queen gave a wan smile. "What about this devoted page Babington?" she asked me.

"He wants to rescue you from here, drive Elizabeth off her throne and put you there in her place."

The Queen's smile faded a little. "There have been ten plots like that. Why should Babington succeed when the others have failed?"

"Because he is English, madam. The other plots were difficult because they were planned in France. This man

◆ 115 ◆

has a small army of followers who know this country well, they can move round freely and not be treated as foreigners. This letter is from France, but it says your friends over there support his plan."

"What do they want me to do?"

"Contact Anthony Babington and tell him to go ahead."

The Queen rose from the edge of the bed where she had been sitting. She was stiff and weak, but some inner strength carried her across the room to the door. She opened it and looked down the corridor. There was no sign of a guard, or a servant of Sir Amyas Paulet. She nodded, satisfied.

"So, Marion. This could be the end of all our suffering!"

The joy in her face was too painful for me to bear. Sir Francis Walsingham had read this secret letter before I had. He knew all about Babington's plot. When the time was right he would arrest everyone. It could never succeed.

The Queen walked slowly across to me and rested her thin hands on my shoulders. "You are going to be busy, Marion. There are lots of letters to write. There is a

London plot to assassinate Elizabeth. We must work with the London assassins – they are just waiting for the word from me to go ahead. Two plots – the escape plot and the assassination plot. You, Marion, Morag and I will control it all through Gifford's secret post. We will be like spiders sitting in the centre of this web."

"And Queen Bess is the fly!" Morag chuckled.

"We will plan it from here. Every detail. We'll be the only ones who know the whole story, so if one part of the plot fails then the other half won't be betrayed. We have to make sure the rescue immediately follows the killing of Elizabeth."

"But if our plans are uncovered?" I asked, desperately afraid. The Queen sensed my fear and thought I was afraid for my own life. But I knew that Walsingham was the real spider and Queen Mary was the fly. He knew everything. My fear was for her, but I couldn't tell her. I just had to hope I could stop her flying into Walsingham's sticky threads.

"Our plans won't be uncovered. We have tested the letter system and it works perfectly. Everything must be in code, of course."

"Codes can be broken," I said.

"Ah, but seals can't be broken," Morag said fiercely. "All the letters we receive have perfect seals. No one can have opened the letters and read them."

A man called Arthur Burton was Walsingham's expert in breaking seals and repairing them so that no one could tell a letter had been opened. He was working with Gilbert Gifford. "What if the brewer betrays us?" I asked.

"We are paying the brewer well," Queen Mary smiled. "If he lets us down he loses his little fortune."

But Walsingham was paying the brewer more money than Queen Mary could ever afford.

"What if there is a spy in your own household?" I asked finally, frantically hoping she would know that I meant it was me.

"We will have to make sure no one knows," the Queen said. "Only Morag and you and I will know what passes between me and the assassins, and me and Babington. It is a terrible secret to keep, Marion, but you have the strength of knowing that God is with you."

It was a terrible secret that I held, all right, but it wasn't the secret that the Queen thought it was. My shoulders drooped in defeat. If I was writing the letters, then at least I could change what they said and maybe wreck the whole plot.

The lives of a queen of Scotland and a queen of England were in the hands of a sixteen-year-old girl. I have never been so afraid in my life. There was no one I could share my fears with – not the skull-headed Sir Francis Walsingham, who would tell me to write exactly what Queen Mary wanted even if it put her neck on a block; not the harsh Sir Amyas Paulet, who would tell me to choose between my two queens; not Gilbert Gifford, who would betray me to save harming one hair of his own head. And not Morag, because I felt she would kill me before she let anyone betray her beloved queen.

I have never been so afraid. I have never been so alone.

CHAPTER THIRTEEN

"Cut out his tongue for cogging"

Moll Frith slapped her leg and cried, "What an amazing story!"

"Could you have done what my daughter-in-law did?" Grandfather asked.

"I couldn't! I never learned to write."

Grandfather shook his head. "I didn't mean *that*, Moll. I meant, could you live among people, take their food and their trust and all the time be cheating them?" His watery blue eyes watched her carefully.

Moll took her knife from her belt and began to pick her teeth with the point. She found a strand of goose flesh, picked it off with her finger and pushed it back in her mouth. "I don't think I could. I'm too *honest*, that's my trouble. If I tried to tell you a lie, you'd know straight away. My honest little face would give me away!" she chuckled. "I wish I could stay a little longer to hear the rest of your story, Marion. Maybe you can tell me how it all ended when you come down to the Black Bull later."

"It's not the sort of story for a noisy mob to hear," my grandmother said sharply. "There are still a lot of people afraid that the Catholics will come back one day. Lady Marsden is well liked in these parts. Some folk may turn nasty if they find she served Mary Queen of Scots. They still remember the terror we suffered at the time."

Moll Frith held up a hand. "You're right ... and of

course her secret is safe with me! Secrets are locked tighter in this head than your silver ship is locked in that cupboard upstairs," she said, her gaze drifting towards the ceiling. "But I have to get back to the tavern. A lot of people are relying on me to find their precious things. I can't let them down."

"And, of course, you make a good living out of it," Grandfather said.

She shook her head sadly. "A few pennies, a few pennies. Michael the Taverner takes most of what I earn!"

I'd watched the money shared out the night before, and knew that wasn't true. Her "honest little face" didn't give her away. I wondered how many other lies she'd told.

"Goodnight!" she called from the doorway. "And thanks for a very tasty meal. Another night of Michael's stewed squirrel would have killed me."

"Stewed squirrel!" I laughed. "He's not that bad!"

"Sorry, Will, my lad. I cannot tell a lie, you know that. But Michael found a dead squirrel in the woods yesterday and skinned it and sold it in his tavern."

"No one would buy roast squirrel!"

"No! But he boiled it up and served it as chicken stew, didn't he? I bought a bowl for a young beggar friend of Meg's, didn't I, Meg?"

"You did," said Meg. She gave a quick glance at me.

"Is your dummerer cousin still alive?" Moll asked.

Meg gave a happy grin. "He enjoyed it!" she said.

"Must have been desperate," Moll muttered as she walked out of the door.

I felt ill again at the memory of that stew and the thought of what I'd eaten. Father always said a squirrel is nothing more than a rat with a bushy tail. Meg had made me eat it. There had to be some way I could get even with her.

"You're not going to that dreadful tavern, are you, Marion?" my grandmother asked. "James can't make you do that just for the sake of a silver cup."

My mother turned to the family and said, "Last night Will went to the tavern dressed as a beggar. James wanted to see what he could find out. He can go back tonight in the same disguise. I'll be happy knowing that he's there."

Grandmother stood up. "James is my own son, but sometimes I feel sorry for you, Marion, being married to him."

"Marriage can be a terrible trial," Grandfather agreed.

"Only for the women," Grandmother snapped back. My grandparents left the hall quarrelling as loudly as ever. I knew that was what made them happy.

Meg took me back to the kitchen to dress me as her beggar cousin again and in half an hour we were ready to follow Moll Frith across to the rats' nest that they called the Black Bull.

My mother took the steward with her to light the way with a lantern while I hung back in the shadows, following behind them. I wore a pair of boots to protect my feet against the frosted ground and left them hidden behind a barrel at the tavern door when I went in.

Michael the Taverner was red-faced and fish-eyed as my mother walked into the tavern. "Ah! Lady Marsden!

So you decided to accept my offer of a cup of my best Rhenish wine, then?"

"No, Master Taverner, I am here to consult with Moll Frith," my mother explained. The noise in the tavern had dropped and the customers were looking at my mother curiously. Some were afraid of her as the wife of the magistrate, and some just wondered what she was doing in this place. No one noticed me as I crept behind her and took my place in a dark corner.

"Our famous Moll!" Michael cried. "She has never failed yet. She is a miracle, that girl. I do believe she may be a saint, sent down from heaven to help us fight this devil thief."

"What devil thief?" my mother asked.

"Why … the one who is doing all this cutting of purses and footpadding in the woods and burglary in the houses," Michael said.

"If Moll is an angel from Heaven, then I think God may have asked her to tell us who the thief is, don't you?"

"As you say, Lady Marsden," said Michael. "Moll has many people waiting to hear her horoscopes tonight. Perhaps you would care to wait in one of my private rooms."

"Thank you," said my mother, and she allowed him to lead her out of a side door into a passageway. I was worried that she was out of my sight, but I couldn't follow her without people becoming suspicious. Michael's horse-stealing friend, Wat Grey, was sitting by the door. The little eyes never stopped scanning the room, even when he was supping from his wine cup.

Moll was talking to a farmer who had lost his purse at Chester-le-Street market that morning. "All winter we've kept that cow and fed it the best hay. My wife and I need the money I got for the cow to feed our little ones."

"How many children do you have, farmer?" Moll asked.

"Eleven," he said. "Seven still alive. But I fear they'll

starve now. Seven more little graves alongside the four in the bottom meadow, and all because some villain stole my purse."

Moll sucked on her pipe and blew a cloud of foul smoke in his face. "Nine more graves, farmer. If your children starve then you and your wife will starve too. That'll be nine graves, won't it?"

The man's eyes were shifty. "What do you mean?"

"You are fat, farmer. If your children are close to starving, it's because you are eating all their food. I've never seen a poor man as fat as you."

"But my purse is gone!" the man complained.

"If it's been stolen," Moll said, "it's probably in a pocket much emptier than yours." She laughed and blew more smoke in his face.

The farmer waved a hand at the brown fog. "Theft is a crime."

"And lying is a crime in the sight of God!" Moll said. She pointed at him with the stem of her pipe. "You're a liar, farmer. I cannot give a true prediction to a man who is untrue. Go away and take some gold from the store under your floorboards. You can afford it."

The man stood up quickly, drained his pot of ale and crashed it down on the table in front of Moll so that the handle snapped off. He turned and barged through the crowd to get out of the room, followed by loud laughter. "Well done, Moll!" someone cried. She waved her pipe at him and grinned.

Michael stepped across to the soothsayer and whispered in her ear. He seemed to be nodding towards the door that my mother had left by. Moll nodded, rose to her feet and followed him into the corridor. "It's my turn next!" a thin woman cried.

"She's just gone to the jakes," Wat Grey said. "She'll be back in a minute or two. Have another drink, Alice."

The woman sat down, grumbling, while Meg hurried over to her side with a jug of ale and filled up the pot. She caught my eye, marched over to me and said loudly. "You're not going to sit there all night, you waster. Come out the back and I'll give you some plates to clean. You won't get another bowl of Michael's lovely chicken stew tonight unless you work for it."

Meg grabbed me roughly by the shoulder and dragged me towards the passage. She closed the door behind me and left us in the quiet gloom. A single tallow candle lit the long corridor and doors led off it into darker rooms. "Listen, Will, your mother is in the second room along. If you sit in the first room, you can make sure she's safe."

"From a separate room?" I asked.

"The walls are made of the thinnest wood. You could even poke a hole through and see what's going on. Hurry up," she urged, leading me into the dark room and sitting me on the floor of rushes. "Now, I have to get back to work before Wat misses me."

She left me and closed the door. The room was cold and damp. It smelled of dead cats and unwashed humans. Something unspeakable rustled in the straw in the far corner. I didn't know if it was a rat or a human guest. I didn't know if it would bite me – whether it was rat or human I was in equal danger. After a few moments the rustling stopped.

Meg was right. I could hear almost everything that was said in the next room.

I used the tip of my knife to gouge a small hole in the panel. I could see my mother sitting at a table facing an empty chair. In a few minutes Moll entered and sat opposite her.

"Tragic loss, Marion. Imagine losing the cup a second time! It's a shame your Jim can't control the footpads in

◆ 124 ◆

his own woods, isn't it? Ha!" she gave a loud laugh.

My mother spoke quietly and politely. "What footpads are those, Moll?"

"Why, footpads like the one that stole his cup the second time," Moll said.

"Who said it was stolen by a footpad in the woods?" my mother went on patiently.

"Why, your husband Jim told me! You were there. Before he went off to bed sick. I asked for the reward and he said he didn't want to pay me because he'd been robbed. You must remember that, Marion."

"I remember it well. Sir James said the cup was stolen from him again."

"See! Like I said."

"But he said nothing about footpads in the woods. It could have been stolen from the house, or he could have left it in the saddle pack on his horse. Why did you say it was a footpad in the wood, Moll?"

Moll sighed. "So how did he lose it this time?" she asked.

"He was robbed by a footpad in the wood," Mother said.

"Amazing!" Moll cried. "That's my magical powers again! My second sight! He didn't tell me how he was robbed, yet I knew! I could see it as plain as if I was there.

I tell you, Marion, this power of mine is so great it frightens me at times." Suddenly she gave a cry of surprise.

"What's wrong?" Mother asked.

"It's like I said! It's as if I'm there now. I can see pictures in the air. He is coming from the river carrying the cup ... there's a footpad standing in the path ... the pad has a club in one hand ... Jim falls to his knees. 'Don't hurt me!' he's crying. 'Take the cup but don't hurt me!' The pad holds out his other hand ... he hands the cup over and the pad runs off. I see a cottage on his left hand."

"That'll be Widow Atkinson's cottage," Mother murmured.

"The pad runs down the path and hides the cup under the thatch on the cottage roof. I see it as plain as day!"

"Why would the footpad do that?"

"In case he gets caught, of course. If Jim recognizes the pad, then the pad can say, 'Search me!' and he'll be clean."

"I see. So the cup is in the thatch of Widow Atkinson's cottage."

"Just above the door," Moll said. "Jim owes me twelve shillings if I'm right!"

"Thank you, Moll," my mother said, rising to her feet. "This time we'll take the constable and a few armed men to collect the cup, shall we?"

"Wat Grey could go and fetch it for you," Moll offered.

"But Wat is as small as Sir James. He could be robbed by this great, ugly brute of a footpad. No, we'll wait till daylight."

"The pad might have taken the cup and disappeared before then."

"True. This villain is having a bad time. Every time he steals something he hides it and you find it before he can sell it. He must be getting really angry with you."

Moll grinned. "Maybe he'll give up and move on to some new patch soon."

"Maybe he'd better," my mother said quietly. Her voice had a soft menace in it. "Otherwise his luck might run out and he might find himself swinging from Marsden gallows." She stood up and went to the door.

Michael Taverner was standing there. "Everything satisfactory, Lady Marsden?" he asked.

"I think so," she said. "Call my steward and I'll go home."

I had to sit quiet for a short time while Michael left the corridor outside my door and Mother went back into the public room. But Moll stayed where she was and Michael came back. "Well?" he asked.

"She's a clever woman, that Marion," Moll chuckled. "She's not as stupid as her husband."

"She suspects you?"

"I think she's worked it out," said Moll.

"You'd better go back to London," said Michael.

"Tomorrow," said Moll. "I've got one last job I want to do before I go."

"You're doing a last job tonight?"

"Tomorrow. You said that everybody goes to the Shrove Tuesday football match, didn't you?"

"That's right."

"So the houses will all be empty?"

"Usually. So, you'll do the job and ride straight off to London?"

"That's what I reckon," Moll said.

"And how do I get my share?"

"I'll drop half the stuff under the bridge when I cross it."

"How do I know I can trust you?"

"Oh, Michael!" she cried. "What a way to treat your partner! Wait by the bridge, if you like. I can't cross it without paying you. How's that?"

"Fine. The football starts at eleven. I'll be there at noon."

"Right!" Moll said. "Let's get back to the public room and see some more customers, shall we?"

The two left the room and everything went quiet. I stood up, stiff from being crouched on the damp floor. I moved to the door and lifted the latch. I looked out into the dim passageway and slipped out. I thought there might be a back entrance to the tavern, but I wasn't sure which way to turn. While I was deciding, the door from the public room flew open and Wat Grey stood there.

"Hello, my little friend! What are you doing here? Trying to go through our guests' rooms and do a bit of thieving, are you?"

I gave a grunt and shook my head as if I didn't understand what he was saying. He looked over my head and saw the open door behind me. "You been in there, have you?" He snatched at my ragged cloak. His hands were bony, but surprisingly strong. He held me and looked back into the public room. "Michael!"

The taverner joined him. "What, Wat?"

The little man glared at the fat taverner. "I told you not to say that!"

"Say what, Wat?"

"Yes!"

"What?"

"Make fun of my name like that."

"What fun?"

"Just stop it!" the horse-thief snapped. "Have you been in your room with Moll?"

"Yes."

"Talking over plans?"

"Yes."

"This little spy was next door all the time!"

"God's nails! That could ruin everything," the taverner hissed. He closed the door of the public room behind him. "What should we do?"

"Cut his throat."

"No one will miss a beggar. We can cut him up and feed him to the pigs," Wat suggested.

"Seems a waste."

"What? You mean you could use him in one of your stews?" Wat Grey asked.

"No! I mean a waste of the fresh rushes I just put down in this passage. Can't you cut his throat in a stable?"

"I thought *you* might like to do it," Wat said.

"What?"

"What?"

"What?"

"You said Wat."

"I said, *what* do you mean? I've never cut a throat in my life."

"Neither have I."

"You've killed pigs and chick-ens, haven't you?"

"Yes."

"Well, it's the same thing."

"So you do it."

"No."

"Why not?"

"It's not the same – murdering a boy."

"You just said it was."

"Can't we just cut his tongue out?"

While the two men argued I had to make a decision. Did I keep my mouth shut and have my throat slit? Or did I tell them I was Will Marsden, the son of their local magistrate? If I told them who I *really* was then they'd be certain I was spying on them. Their crimes would see them hang, so they would have to kill me.

I remember my mother had said that Mary Queen of Scots was offered the chance to die as a Protestant, but chose to be true to herself and die as a Catholic.

That was my choice too, in a way. Die as a dummerer, or be true to myself and die as Will Marsden.

Apart from the problem of choosing I had another problem. I didn't really want to die at all.

CHAPTER FOURTEEN

"Away, you cutpurse rascal, you filthy bung, away!"

"What are you doing?" the voice asked.

The door behind Michael Taverner had opened. Michael swung round and I saw Meg standing behind him. He was already upset by the argument over my murder. He took out his temper on the girl. "It's your miserable little cousin here. You brought him into this place and you ought to have taken better care of him. It's not our fault if he ends up dead, is it, Wat?"

"No. The brat deserves everything he gets."

"What's he done?" Meg asked, staying calm.

"Hidden in this room," Michael said. "He must have overheard some very secret words I had with Mo ... my friend. I can't let him go babbling to the magistrate and anyone else in the village. It's more than my life's worth."

"How did he hear your plans?" Meg asked.

"He listened at the wall, didn't he?"

"A deaf-and-dumb boy listened to your plans?"

"Yes."

"How could he do that if he's deaf?"

Michael and Wat suddenly went quiet. They looked at one another foolishly. Finally Michael cleared his throat. "How could a deaf boy hear us, Wat?" Michael asked fiercely. "You forgot that he was deaf, didn't you? Eh? Didn't you?"

"Me? What about you?"

"It's your fault, you louse-brain. Coming running to me with stories of spies."

Wat Grey wiped a snivelling nose on his sleeve. "It was you that wanted me to cut his throat. Just as well I refused, isn't it?"

Meg raised her voice. "My cousin heard nothing and he won't be saying anything. Now, if it's all right with you I'll show him to a nice warm stable at Marsden Hall."

"Aye, you do that, lass. But there's still a lot of serving to be done. The place is crowded tonight." The taverner wiped his sweating hands on his greasy apron and went back into the public room, followed by a grumbling Wat Grey.

Meg pushed my hood back. Even in the light of the single tallow candle her eyes were sparkling with excitement. "How many times do I have to save your life, Master Marsden?" she asked.

"Thanks, Meg," I mumbled.

"Perhaps you can do the same for me some day."

Knowing my father's plans for her, I hoped I could. "I know who stole the cup," I said.

"Stole the cup from the kitchen of Marsden Hall? Or stole the cup from your father in the woods?"

"Both," I said. "And I know who's been cutting purses in Chester-le-Street market and robbing farmers in Bournmoor Woods and burgling houses."

Meg looked round nervously. "Not here, Will," she said. "These walls are thin and we don't know who might be listening. We'll go out the back way and get you back to Marsden Hall."

"My boots are hidden at the front," I said.

"I'll get them later," she said. "I'll be back in Marsden Hall when the tavern closes. Will you wait up for me?"

"I will," I promised.

Meg led me along the maze of passages and finally to a

door that led out on to the church road. Ice numbed my feet as I struggled over the road towards Marsden Hall. A half moon showed the high wall that surrounded the house. I found the gateway, limped up the coach path to the side of the house, let myself in through the kitchen door and went up the servants' stairway to my room.

When I was dressed in clean, warm hose and had washed the disguise off my face I went downstairs to the main hall. My mother was sitting by the hearth. Most of the ash was grey now, but the hearthstones still threw off a welcome heat.

"There you are, Will," she smiled. "I was worried."

"Not so worried as I was about you. I thought you were in danger when you were talking to Moll Frith. I thought she might try to silence you."

"No. Moll is clever and wicked, but I don't think she's a murderer. I don't think she'd kill me to keep me quiet."

"How do you know?"

"Because I've met killers, remember? I was more in fear of my life when I was serving Mary Queen of Scots. If I'd been caught then, I'm sure Queen Mary would have been happy to order my murder. After all, she was cold-blooded enough to order the assassination of her own cousin, Queen Elizabeth."

I remembered the argument between Wat Grey and Michael Taverner. "But it's easier to order a murder than it is to do it. Queen Mary would never have hurt you herself."

"Maybe not," my mother agreed. "But I wasn't so sure about Morag. I was sure that Morag would have done anything to defend her queen. I believed she'd have pushed a knife between my ribs and smiled as she did it."

"So how did you keep yourself safe?"

My mother stirred the ashes and spread them over the hearth. Then she began to make marks in the ash with the tip of the poker. "I did as the Queen asked. I wrote the letters she wanted and read the replies as they came in. For the first few months the letters were harmless enough: Queen Mary writing and complaining about her health and about Sir Amyas Paulet. She moaned about her lack of money and how few servants she now had to help her. There was nothing for Sir Francis Walsingham to worry about until the Anthony Babington plot came along."

"What are the marks you're making in the ash?" I asked.

"I'm trying to see if I still remember the code we used."

"I have my pen and ink here," I said, going to the table. "Can I make a copy?"

My mother went on working in the ash until she was satisfied. "Yes. This is it," she said finally.

I copied the code carefully. I've always been interested in writing and the way marks on a piece of paper can change people's lives. Queen Mary's code was a simple mixture of shapes and Greek letters. Each shape made a letter and some shapes made the most common words. I still have the code and I take it out from time to time to look at it.

I could see at once that it was too simple. Even if I didn't have the code I could have started understanding messages after an hour or two. And Walsingham had the code anyway.

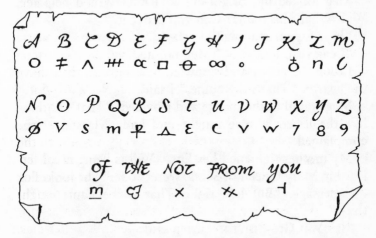

For an hour or so I wrote messages in the ash and my mother replied. After a while I no longer needed to use my copy of the code. I imagined Gifford and Walsingham had become expert after a while too.

It was round midnight, when the timbers of the old house were creaking and settling for the night, that Meg came back.

"I've never seen so many people in the Black Bull," she said. "No wonder Michael needed help."

"Sit down, Meg," my mother said. "We need to talk about these robberies."

The girl sank on to the hearthstone and rested her back against the heavy stone fireplace. "There's something going on in the Black Bull, but I can't work out what it is. I think there's a thief come into the area and he's stealing everything he can get his hands on. But Moll Frith and Michael Taverner and Wat Grey are making the most money out of him. Sorry, I haven't seen the thief and no one's let his name slip."

"I think we may be able to help," my mother said. "I think Will knows the name of the thief."

Meg looked up, bright-eyed, "I knew you'd help me, Will. What's his name? Can you prove it?"

"How's your reading?" I asked.

"I can read lots now," Meg boasted.

I took the poker and scrawled nine signs in the ash on the hearth. "That's the name," I said.

Meg stared at the marks and frowned. "That's nothing like the letters you've taught me, Lady Marsden," she complained.

My mother tightened her lips. "Will is being cruel. He is using Mary Queen of Scots' secret code." She looked at the message. "But he's right. That is the name of the thief."

"It's Wat Grey, isn't it?" Meg said.

"Wat's too small. Father said it was a large man who attacked him."

"Michael Taverner, then?"

"No. Michael was talking to you in the garden when the cup was stolen the first time."

"Then who?"

I looked at my mother. She gave a tiny nod in my direction.

"It's Moll Frith," I said.

Meg's mouth fell open. "That doesn't make sense. She risks everything to steal these things, then she helps people to get them back! Is she mad?"

"Not at all," my mother told her. "It's a clever scheme. You see, it's easy enough to steal something like our silver cup, but it's very hard to sell it. The thief can't take it to a silversmith because the smith will want to know where a girl like her got a cup like that. She'd be arrested. And if she takes it to a dealer in stolen goods, he'll give her just a few shillings for it. Stealing is easy – getting money back for stolen property is very hard."

Meg nodded excitedly. "I see, I see! So she hides the cup and pretends to know where the thief has hidden it. That way she gets a good reward and there's nothing to link her to the robbery." Meg thought for a while. "So why did she steal Sir James's cup a second time?"

"Because she enjoys her work," my mother said. "It was daring and exciting to steal the cup from the kitchen. But to let Sir James dabble in freezing water for an hour, then steal it from him a second time, was just a wonderful joke to a woman like Moll Frith."

"Can you prove it?" Meg asked.

"I don't think so," my mother admitted.

"Can't you stop her?"

"I hinted that I knew what she was up to when I met her tonight. She got careless and almost gave herself away. But that hasn't stopped her," said my mother.

"But it has," I told her. "When you left I heard her telling Michael that she'd leave tomorrow – she'll be leaving after she's done one last job."

"What is she planning to steal?"

"I don't know," I said. "Something from a house. She said something about all the houses being empty when the football match starts at eleven o'clock."

"Pity we don't know more," Meg said. "We could catch her in the act and prove she's guilty."

"Catch her and she'll hang," I said quickly. "Remember, Father swore that the person who robbed him down by the river will hang, and he meant it. Do you want that?"

Meg shook her head. "Not really. I suppose it would be best if we could prove she's guilty and then let her escape."

"We could watch her when the football starts and follow wherever she goes," I suggested. "That's all I can think of at the moment."

My mother and Meg were frowning, but neither could come up with a better idea. Meg placed her hands over her eyes, rubbed them and yawned. "I think I need some sleep," she said.

"I think we all do. Tomorrow will be a busy day."

Meg stared bleakly towards the blackness beyond the windows. "Tomorrow would be my last day if Sir James had his way."

"But he doesn't always get his way," my mother said gently.

"Not always," I thought. "But usually."

The whole family rose early the next morning and went to church for the Shrove Tuesday service, all in our finest clothes. We sat in the front row where everyone in the village could see us. It was a way of reminding everyone of our place in the manor.

I noticed for the first time that my mother took as little part in the service as possible. Her lips moved during the prayers, but she wasn't saying the words of the Protestant Prayer Book. I could see how she had got away with it for so long. The congregation was behind her and only the priest in front, and he was too busy reading.

We were the first to leave after the service, following the priest down the aisle to the exit at the back of the church. I was used to the people of the manor staring at us as we walked in procession, some faces curious, some envious and some trying hard to catch my father's eye with a humble smile.

"I will see you again at eleven o'clock," my father promised the priest.

"Ah, yes," said the priest, folding his hands together as if he were still in prayer. "The football match. I hope no one is killed this year. Such a violent game."

"The honour of Marsden Manor depends on it," my father said, waving a finger under the priest's nose. "We can't have Lord Birtley smirking for the rest of the year about his village's victory over mine."

"No, Sir James. We don't win as often as we used to."

Father's neck stretched proudly over his ruff. "Marsden men must be made afraid of what will happen if they lose," he said.

"Will your son be taking part?" the priest asked.

"Certainly not. It's a sport for ruffians and cutthroats. My son is neither."

"Of course not, Sir James," the priest said, cringing.

When we reached home the stolen cup was on the table in the great hall. My mother presented my father with it and said, "The girl fetched it from its hiding place."

"She probably put it there," he sneered.

"The thief put it there," my mother said. "It wasn't Meg who robbed you on the path, was it?"

"Of course not!"

"Moll Frith told me last night where the thief had hidden the cup and I sent Meg to get it this morning. Now will you remove this terrible threat to hang the girl?"

My father's ferret face closed hard and ugly like one of the carved stone faces on the gutters of Durham Cathedral. "No." He stalked out of the room.

My mother sighed. She looked worried as Meg came into the room and brightly told us there was a woman at the back door who said she was a dressmaker. "Show her in," said my mother.

The dressmaker came in with a parcel wrapped in dark cloth. She laid it on the table, opened it carefully, and held up the dress to the light. The wool was fine, its colour a rich green. Small gold buttons decorated the cuffs and the front. A neat lace ruff was sewn into the neck.

My mother asked, "What do you think, Meg?"

"It's much too small for you, madam!"

"The dress isn't for me, Meg. It's for you."

"I can't afford a dress like that!"

"No, but I can. I'm buying it for you."

"But – why?"

My mother could see that Meg was struggling with the idea of receiving a present when she'd probably never had one in her life. "I've never had my own maidservant, Meg. I believe that a lady of the manor should have one. I'd like to teach you to be a lady's maid. But a lady is judged by her servants, you know. It wouldn't do for me to be seen with a girl in a faded black dress."

The explanation seemed to satisfy Meg. She couldn't take

her eyes off the dress. Her mouth opened and closed again as she struggled to find words.

"Don't you like it?" I asked awkwardly.

Her sea-green eyes filled with tears and rolled down her pale cheeks. "It's the loveliest thing I've ever seen."

The dressmaker and my mother looked pleased. Meg just shook her head and wiped her eyes with the back of her wrist.

"Aren't you going to try it on?" I asked.

"Elise will take Meg to my room and fit it properly, won't you?"

The dressmaker nodded and picked up the dress and a small workbasket. Meg led the way out of the room. I'd never known her so quiet.

"Does she really like it?" I asked.

"I think so."

"So why is she crying?"

"Because she's happy," my mother explained.

I stared at her. "And why are you crying?" I asked.

"You ask too many questions," she said.

CHAPTER FIFTEEN

"Till the axe of death hang over thee, as sure it shortly will"

"Your spying worked, then," said my mother.

"But Meg's not safe yet. Not until I can prove that Moll Frith is the thief. How can I do that?" I asked.

My mother looked across the frosted grass. Our footprints stood out clearly as grey-green shadows on the white background. "We can't prove Moll stole the cup," she said, "but we can prove that she is a thief."

"I don't understand," I said.

"We need to be ready for her when she makes her last big robbery attempt today."

"I said we should follow her today. You and Meg didn't think it was such a good idea."

"No. Moll is too clever to be caught that way. And she's too clever to be caught in a trap if someone is waiting for her. We need to let her commit the crime and steal the goods and then catch her."

"We'd need to know where she planned to rob," I said.

"We can guess."

"But we need to prove that she was the thief."

"Look at the grass, Will," my mother said.

I stared at it for a long time. At last I understood. "Yes," I said. "It's risky. But we can do it." I grinned at her. "Where did you learn to be such a good thief-taker?"

She didn't smile back. "I spent over a year with Mary Queen of Scots learning all the tricks and traps to catch people. Traitors like Babington."

"What was he like?"

"I never met him, of course, but he was said to be an attractive young man. He was rich and had lots of friends. Catholics gathered round him the way pieces of iron gather round a magnet. He was very clever, but he was desperate for adventure. The greatest adventure for a Catholic would be to set Queen Mary free, of course. I was with Queen Mary when we opened his first letter in the summer of 1586 ..."

LADY MARSDEN'S STORY

"There is a letter in the beer barrel, madam," I said.

Morag was brushing the Queen's hair and looked at me suspiciously. She hated the way the Queen trusted me with the letters. "Another letter from France?" she asked.

"No. This is from our friend Sir Anthony Babington of Derbyshire."

"And what does he want?"

I began decoding the letter and felt a shudder of fear. I knew that Walsingham had already seen it and Master Babington was writing his own death warrant. "He says he has gathered a group of supporters in London. They know about the plot to assassinate Queen Elizabeth."

"Ballard's plot," Morag said.

"Babington is also in touch with your friends in Spain and France. A force is being put together to invade England," I said.

"A large enough force?" the Queen asked.

"Large enough, Babington says. But he has armed groups organized all over England. Once the invasion starts, the English Catholics will rise up and take over their counties. Elizabeth can't fight a foreign army and a dozen civil wars, he says."

"What else does he say?"

"He says that he himself will lead a company of a hundred trusted friends and set you free from Chartley."

"Sir Amyas Paulet doesn't have a hundred men to defend the place," Morag said. "He'll surrender."

"I hope not," the Queen said viciously. "I hope he fights to the death." She turned back to me. "But what about the woman who's stolen my throne? What will he do about Elizabeth?"

"There's a group of six noble gentlemen – all Babington's trusted friends – they'll make sure that Queen Elizabeth dies as soon as the invasion is successful and you are free."

The letter gave a lot of detail on the plans and I passed them on faithfully to the Queen.

"I have heard of plots like this before," the Queen said. "I have never given my support to plans like this in the past. That would give cousin Elizabeth the excuse she needs to execute me."

Morag fell on her knees in front of the Queen. "You are not well, madam. You need your freedom, or you will die. This is your best chance of taking that dreadful woman's throne. It may be your last chance."

The Queen stroked the girl's dark hair and looked across to me. "And you, Marion? What do you say?"

"If the plan fails, and your letter falls into the hands of Walsingham and the Queen, she will never let you live."

Queen Mary was about to reply, but Morag jumped to her feet. "Coward, Marion. You're a coward! If you risk nothing, you win nothing!"

"And you lose nothing," I said, trying to stay calm. "It's Queen Mary's life you want to gamble with."

Morag took quick steps towards me till her face was close to mine. "No. It's my own life too. If the plot fails we'll all be executed. But I'm ready to die for my queen. You're not. You're a coward. A feeble, crawling coward."

"Morag," the Queen said sharply. "We mustn't fight amongst ourselves. Marion doesn't have to prove her courage to anyone. She did that at Lyford Grange six years ago. I need to hear calm, reasonable arguments."

Morag turned back, distressed. "Oh, I'm sorry, madam," she groaned. "I care so much. I want to see you free. I'm desperate!" She fell on her knees again by the Queen and buried her face in the rich red velvet folds of her dress.

The Queen looked at me. "I will decide tomorrow. After a night's sleep I will be ready to reply."

I knew what the reply would be. Queen Mary had been a prisoner too long. Every year that passed made her more reckless, more frantic to find a way out of her miserable existence whatever the cost.

We sat in a high tower room looking out over the lilies in the lake around Chartley. The distant hills and woods were bursting with summer green while we were trapped inside the grim grey walls. Queen Mary wanted to be hunting in those woods, rowing on the lake amongst the lilies, and living in a palace, not a prison. I couldn't blame her. Yet I couldn't tell her that this was not the way to achieve her dream.

"We will reply to Anthony Babington," she said.

Morag had a look of fierce happiness on her face. Her glance at me was one of triumph.

It took us all that day to prepare the reply and then put it into the code. Queen Mary fretted over details. She wanted Babington to place guards round Chartley so that news of Elizabeth's death didn't get through to Paulet. If it did, she feared her jailer would move her or even kill her.

A little of my concern went into the letter. The Queen told her rescuers to risk nothing until the foreign invasion was certain. It was a warning. It was useless, as I knew it would be.

The Queen opened the lid of her sewing box and said, "Put the letter at the bottom of this box. Paulet never searches that."

Queen Mary had spoken the words, but I had written them down. I had written words that would lead to the deaths of many people. Not wicked people. Just foolish people. There was only one thing I could do.

When the Queen went to bed that night I lay in the darkness and listened to the sounds of the night outside my open window. Owls cried in the distant woods and ducks squabbled on the lake below. But I was listening for another sound. Morag breathed softly on the bed beside me and, when I was sure she was asleep, I

slipped out from under the covers, put on a robe and crept across to the door.

The door had been stiff and creaking, but I'd greased the latch and the hinge with a little fat from the duck we had had for dinner, and so it opened silently.

The door to the sewing room creaked, but it didn't matter. There was no one within earshot. I struck a flint to light a candle and opened the sewing box, took the letter out and read it again. Then I took my writing tools and started work on another letter. A letter in code to Babington – a letter that I knew Walsingham would read.

I longed to write and warn Babington, but I knew my parents and brothers would go to the torture chambers of the Tower as soon as the Queen's secretary read them. So I forged a letter from Queen Mary. I still have it.

My mother stopped her story and pulled a letter from a deep pocket in her dress and passed it to me.

I recognized the code as the one she'd taught me last night and read it almost as easily as if it had been written in English.

"That's clever," I said. "Very clever. That's the letter Queen Mary should have written. It would have spoiled all Walsingham's plans. It would have saved Queen Mary's life."

"That's what I thought," said my mother.

"What went wrong?"

My dear Sir Anthony Babington

I thank you for your letter with details of the plot you propose. It warms my heart to know that there are so many loyal friends in the world who want to risk all for my freedom.

There is one major fault in your plan, however. My cousin Elizabeth will never give up her throne to me. She would have to die before I could become Queen of England. I cannot allow you to murder a rightful queen, even though she is not a Catholic. You say the Pope will forgive you. But I could never forgive myself and I could never sit on a throne that is stained with the blood of my cousin.

You and your loyal friends must work for the freedom of the Catholic people in England, show that Catholics can be loyal to Elizabeth and stay Catholic. That way you may win the freedom to worship in our church. But plot to kill Elizabeth and the Protestants will never forgive us. We will be persecuted forever.

The great plot must not go ahead.
This is the order of your true Queen

MarieR

LADY MARSDEN'S STORY

I finished the letter and was starting to fold it when I sensed a movement in the doorway. I don't know how long she'd been standing there.

"What are you doing?" Morag asked. She held a knife in her hand. The blade shone in the light of my candle. It was pointed at my throat.

"Morag, sit down," I told her.

She sat on the Queen's chair and looked at me with a cold gaze. The knife rested on her knee, her hand wrapped round it tightly and the blade still in my direction. "Well?"

"Morag ... I don't trust Gilbert Gifford."

"He's a Catholic, isn't he?"

"Yes ... but he is also a weak man. Don't you think it's strange that all Queen Elizabeth's spies have failed to stop the beer-barrel letters?"

"No. It's a clever scheme."

I didn't want to tell her the whole truth for I was sure she'd kill me. I invented a story. "My father says Gifford is not to be trusted. He says Gifford was seen visiting Sir Francis Walsingham in London."

Morag's eyes moved to the letter and then back to my face. "Why didn't you tell the Queen."

"It would break her spirit if she has another disappointment. You've seen how happy she is to be plotting her freedom. We have to find a safe way to write to Babington – a really safe way."

"And in the meantime?"

"Don't send anything that might give Elizabeth an excuse to execute our queen."

"What were you writing?"

"A reply to Babington."

"Read it to me."

I read my letter to Morag and she listened carefully. When I'd finished she slipped the knife into the belt of her night robe and gave a sly smile. "Give me the real letter and put your letter in the bottom of the sewing box," she said.

I handed the letter to her.

"You've done well, Marion. One day the Queen will be grateful."

"I hope so," I said.

"Now we'd better get back to bed. The night guard will be checking our apartments soon. It wouldn't do for him to find this letter, would it?" she asked waving the packet at me.

We went back to bed. I lay awake for a long time while Morag soon began her steady, slow breathing. At last I fell into a deep and dreamless sleep.

The morning sun was high and slanting through the window when I woke. Morag was dressed and smiling down at me. "You had a busy night last night," she said. "I made your excuses to the Queen. But she's anxious for you to deliver that letter. The beer wagon is crossing the causeway now."

I dressed quickly, brushed my hair and ran to the sewing room where Queen Mary was sitting in the warm sunlight working on a tapestry. She watched my every movement as I opened the sewing box and took the letter out. I hurried down the cool corridors and winding stairways of Chartley till I reached the basement.

Gifford was waiting in the beer cellars. I handed him the letter and he began rolling it carefully to fit in the secret compartment. "Has she agreed to the Babington plot?" he asked.

"She has," I told him.

"Then she has walked into Walsingham's trap," he said gleefully. It was hard to remember the young Catholic who had been prepared to fight for Queen Mary. Of all the traitors, I sometimes thought Gifford was the most loathsome. At other times I knew it was I myself.

"When will you bring the next letters?" I asked.

"I won't," he said. "My work is finished now. I leave for France tomorrow."

I wished that I could have escaped that easily. I knew that Walsingham still had work for me to do.

The day the Babington letter left, the Queen felt well enough to be carried in a chair down to the lake side where she watched duck shooting. Sir Amyas Paulet mentioned that she seemed in good spirits. He pretended to be surprised. He knew as well as I did that it was hope of freedom that raised the Queen's spirits.

The month after the Babington letter was sent was the only happy time I knew with the Queen. Her health and spirits were so much better. She was sure that Babington would rescue her and by the end of the year she'd be Queen of England.

Morag was just as pleased with herself and spent hours talking with the Queen of Scots about her plans for England after the death of Queen Elizabeth. The girl still didn't seem to like or trust me, but she shared her dreams with me. "I'll be Her Majesty's chief lady-in-waiting, when she takes Elizabeth's throne. Every rich and handsome man in the country will want my hand in marriage. And you'll be my companion, Marion," she promised. "When I've chosen my husband you can have the next best one. He is still likely to be a great gentleman, though."

"Thank you, Morag," I said. I knew it would never come to that. I knew that the Babington plot would fail and the Queen would never take Elizabeth's crown. But I was still caught up in the happy spirit of the prison. The worst that could happen would be that the Queen was sent into exile in France. But that was the best thing that could happen to her. She could live in a healthier climate, worship in a Catholic church. Best of all she'd be free.

Sir Amyas Paulet began to thaw towards us in the summer days after the letter went. One day he came to us and asked if the Queen would like to go hunting with him.

The Queen was thrilled at the idea and had Morag and me running round wildly for an hour making sure every detail of her riding dress was clean and brushed. "After all," she said, "we may meet some of the local gentlemen." She smiled like a girl going to her first meeting with a young man.

We were allowed to choose our horses from Paulet's stable and Queen Mary chose the most spirited. As we rode out of Chartley it was the most glorious August day anyone could have wished for. The thought of endless days like these were what had kept the Queen going for all those years.

Paulet seemed to lag behind. "He's been ill," the Queen told us. "We'll slow down a little to let him keep up."

Paulet was still behind when we saw the horsemen. Four men, riding at speed across the moors towards us. "The rescue!" the Queen gasped.

For a minute I believed her. I was confused and afraid. Maybe Babington had slipped through Walsingham's web and come to free the Queen. The leading rider drew to a halt in front of her. Paulet climbed down and walked towards the man, shook his hand and turned back to the Queen. "This is Sir Thomas Gorges, Queen Elizabeth's messenger."

Sir Thomas dismounted and walked over to Queen Mary who sat like a statue in her saddle. "Madam," he

said, "the Queen my mistress finds it strange that you
have broken your promise and have plotted against her
life. She would not have believed this if she had not seen
the letter with her own eyes."

The Queen's only movement was a slight upward jerk
of the chin. She knew which letter Sir Thomas meant – but
I didn't. Because I had switched the letters to save her life.
Something had gone wrong with my plan and now I faced
the terror of being helpless while my mistress went into
danger.

"I have been loyal to my cousin," the Queen said.

"You have betrayed her and so have your servants,"
said Sir Thomas, nodding towards us. "You will come
with me now to Tixall."

"To be executed?" the Queen gasped.

"You will be held there and taken to a place of trial."

Sir Amyas looked at her calmly. Her face dissolved into
a mask of murderous hatred. "You knew about this,
Paulet. You knew."

Sir Amyas climbed slowly back on to his horse. He

grasped the reins of my horse and Morag's and led us back to Chartley.

"Why did you do that?" Morag asked him.

"If you want to destroy a person then first you take them up to the top of the mountain they call 'Hope'. Just when they think they can see the sun rising on a glorious future you push them off. Your queen will be crushed. She deserves it." He looked me in the eye. "Doesn't she?"

I had no answer.

CHAPTER SIXTEEN

"O, torture me no more
– I will confess"

My father interrupted my mother's story to tell her it was almost eleven o'clock and we had to go with him to the crossroads between Birtley Village and Marsden Village to start the football game.

"James," my mother said, "you are one of the great landowners in this county."

"True," my father nodded. His bent back straightened a little.

"You are always seen in public with your steward."

"A great man shows his wealth by the servants he has."

"And Lord Birtley shows his wealth by having servants for his wife too," my mother said. "So it would be a matter of great pride if I took a maid with me today."

"We haven't got one. I'll see to it after Easter. Maybe some great family has a daughter they want educated in our humble household ... humble, but great, that is."

"I thought I could take Meg with me today," my mother said.

"What? What possible pride could there be in having a ragged kitchen maid alongside you? Especially a thieving kitchen maid condemned to die on the gallows!"

"She's not ragged any more; I used some of my father's money to buy her a dress." Mother walked to the door and came back a minute later with Meg. She was dressed in the gown that went with the green of her eyes. Her hair had been combed and pulled back into a bow of the same green material. Meg folded her hands in front of her and looked meekly at the floor. Until that moment I'd thought my mother was the most beautiful woman I'd ever seen.

Even my father was stunned. He turned and walked out of the door saying, "Very well, but hurry. I don't want to be late!"

"Go with him!" I urged my mother. "I'll catch up in a minute."

I ran to the kitchen and collected a bowl of flour. Then I hurried up the stairs and scattered the flour over the floor of the corridor leading from a cupboard door. I left the house by the kitchen door, turned the key in the lock and ran through the garden to catch up with Meg and my mother.

They were going through the gate that led on to the path through Marsden Village. Meg had a bounce in her walk and Mother looked happier than I'd ever seen her. I felt uneasy because she'd told me that Queen Mary was happiest just before her arrest. I hoped they weren't climbing a mountain called "Hope" only to be thrown off the top. If my father executed Meg and pushed them down, then I knew I would be destroyed along with them. All "Hope" rested on a bowl of flour.

As we walked through the village, the craftsmen and their apprentices fell into line behind us. They were excited about the game ahead and even seemed to look kindly upon my father. "We'll win for Marsden, Sir James!" Robyn the Blacksmith roared, and the others cheered.

Women and children joined the procession and it seemed the whole village was following. It was a holiday, and the weather was fine though cold. A lot of the villagers had warmed themselves with mulled wine at the Black Bull. Michael looked smug as we walked past his tavern. He was juggling a fat purse in his hand. Moll

watched us from a seat by the door, sucking on her pipe. Wat Grey stood in the archway that led to the stables at the back of the tavern. He held a sturdy chestnut horse that was saddled and ready to ride. Behind the saddle were two large leather saddle packs. They lay flat against the horse's quarters, empty. I knew that in an hour's time they'd be full, I knew what would be in them, and I knew who would be riding away with a rich haul.

The frozen ground was softening a little and thawing frost dripped off the bare trees along the side of the road to the north. When we reached the crossroads the villagers from Birtley Manor were already there. Men and boys in leather jerkins scowled across at us and started calling threats and insults. Marsden supporters shouted back while our family walked to the cross in the middle of the road and met the Birtley family.

"You've lost two years in a row, Sir James," said Lord Birtley. "I think it could be three in a row this year. My men are very determined."

"But my men have been practising," Father said slyly. "Robyn the Blacksmith has been training them. Anyway, I told them all the rents would go up a shilling a week if we lose this year."

Lord Birtley laughed and handed my father a bundle about the size of a man's head. Father unwrapped the wooden ball very carefully. It was covered in pig's grease and smelled foul. He held up the ball with the cloth still covering his hand and the baying crowds fell silent.

"Welcome to the Shrove Tuesday football match!" he cried. "Before we start I would just like to say a few words."

"Oh, no!" someone from Birtley cried. There were sniggers from some of the Marsden players.

"I wish to remind you of the rules," my father shouted, turning pink with the effort.

"There aren't any!" someone from Birtley called back.

"The winner is the team who have the ball inside their parish boundaries two hours from now. A pistol shot will signal the end of the game. Remember there must be no weapons used ..."

"What, not even a lump of wood?" someone asked.

"No weapons of any kind," my father said sternly. "And not more force than is necessary to win the ball. Remember, all players must be fit to work tomorrow!"

This was met by a large groan from both sides.

"A man who has his nose broken, or his ear torn off will not be able to earn money – so don't go breaking noses or tearing off ears. I regret to say that both these things happened last year!"

"Can you speak up, Sir James?" someone shouted. "I can't hear you 'cos me ear's been torn off!"

This time there was a roar of laughter from both teams and their supporters.

Father's mouth was tight and thin with anger. "Let us see some gentlemanly behaviour from both sets of players. There is no need for the spectators to spit or use foul language to the opposition. Finally, may I express the hope that the best team wins!"

"So long as it's Marsden!" a woman shouted. Her cry was met with a huge cheer from the hundred players and the two hundred supporters on the Marsden side.

"No one moves until this ball touches the ground!" Father shouted, raising the ball above his head.

Players from both sides began to shuffle forward. I grabbed my mother and Meg and dragged them down the Durham road out of the way. I could see what was going to happen. I turned to see my father shouting, "I haven't released the ball yet!" But the Marsden players took a step nearer to him and the Birtley players thought they should step forward too. Still my father tried to send them back to their road ends and still they ignored him. He held the greasy ball high above his head. Two hundred pairs of eyes were fixed on it. There was a brief silence and then a shout of, "Get it, lads!"

I heard the cry, "I haven't dropped it yet!" but couldn't see my father for the sudden swirl of rushing bodies round him. Someone knocked the ball from his hand. It fell to the ground and twenty men and boys dived for it. Another hundred seemed to ignore the ball and picked someone on the opposite side to punch or kick.

"The Battle of Flodden Field was never this violent," my mother shuddered.

The mass swayed and the spectators screamed. It seemed that a Birtley apprentice boy had the ball hidden up his shirt. He raced off up the road to Birtley while the rest of his team blocked the road and stopped the Marsden men from getting at him. The Marsden players crashed through the hedges to run in the fields and get round the Birtley blocking movement. Women watching from behind the hedge lashed at them with horsewhips and tripped them with sticks.

The Marsden women saw this and set upon the Birtley women, screaming and tearing at them. I saw a woman with a child in her arms holding it up as a shield, while she battered a way through the opposition supporters so a man could get through after her.

The mob rolled away in the direction of Birtley and left behind the sad and battered figure of my father, clinging to the cross at the meeting of the roads. His black fur-trimmed robe was stained with mud, his hat had been torn and he clutched at a swelling eye. "They didn't wait till I dropped it. We really ought to start the game again!" he groaned as he limped towards us.

"Shall I go and get the ball back?" Meg asked. She was looking ladylike, but the spark in her eye said that she wouldn't mind joining in the game herself as she always had in the past.

"We'll leave it for now. But I will protest to Lord Birtley. It was his team that started creeping forward before I gave the signal."

Lord Birtley and his family had been safely out of the way on the Newcastle road. Now he wandered down towards us. "May I invite you to share some mulled wine at Birtley Hall?" he asked. "I believe it's my turn to entertain this year."

My father glared at him and said, "It is. Let's go, Marion. Come along, Will."

"There's something I need to do back home."

"What's that?"

"Some studying, Father. Master Benton has asked me to do a Bible reading in tomorrow's Ash Wednesday Service. I really need to practise."

My father sniffed. "Very well, boy. Be back here for the end of the football game in two hours' time."

"Yes, Father," I promised.

I waited while he walked off with Mother, Meg and the Birtley family. Instead of heading back to our house by the village road I began walking down the Durham road. I didn't want anyone in the village to see me returning. It would spoil my whole plan. I walked south towards Chester-le-Street and turned east on the Wearmouth road. This path would take me through Bournmoor Woods and back to the edge of the village.

I passed Widow Atkinson's cottage and saw her carrying turf from a hut towards her cottage. "Not at the football, young Will?" she asked.

Although she was as old as Grandfather, her brown skin was as shining and healthy as that of a woman half her age. Some villagers said she did it with witchcraft, but I knew it was the clever way she used herbs to keep herself healthy.

"I've got more important things to do," I said.

"I heard your friend Meg's in trouble," she said quietly.

"Not if I can help her," I replied.

"Aye. She'll be all right with you to help her, Will Marsden," she smiled.

"You won't tell anyone you've seen me this morning, will you?"

"Not if it will help," she said.

"Thanks." I turned away and began walking towards the bridge over the Wear with half a plan in my head. I stopped. "Widow Atkinson?" I called.

"Yes, Master Will?"

"Could I borrow your turf hut for half an hour?"

"For what?"

"As a sort of prison," I said.

She thought about it. "There's no lock or bolt on the door," she said. "But you could put someone inside and put a few turves to block the door. They'd never get it open till you took the turf away."

"That's a great help. I'll be back in a little while."

I hurried down the path to the bridge, relieved to see it was deserted. The river ran deep and slow here. The bridge was made of heavy oak beams set on three stone pillars. At each end the beams rested on the river bank and left a small space underneath where someone could hide. I slipped under the beams and tried to stop myself sliding down into the freezing river.

I had a long, cold wait. After a time I began to think that my victims wouldn't turn up and my plans would fail. At last I looked out from my hiding place and saw a pair of grease-stained boots pacing aross the path. He'd arrived so quietly that I hadn't heard his feet on the soft ground.

He was looking up the path to the village, as I knew he would be. I crept out from under the bridge, drew my sword as quietly as I could and tapped him on the shoulder with it. "Good morning, Michael," I said.

He turned so quickly he almost sliced his neck on my sword. His ugly face was white with shock under the dirt. "Master Will!" he croaked. "You nearly scared the life out of me!"

"What a loss that would be to Marsden." I said. I kept the sword pointed at his throat.

He licked his lips and half-turned his head as if he were listening for something coming down the path from the village. "I was just on my way to Chester-le-Street," he said.

"No, you weren't."

"Durham, I mean."

"Liar."

His eyes were small and evil as a wild boar's. They looked at me angrily. "I wasn't doing any harm," he said.

"You were last night," I said.

"Last night?"

"You found a harmless little beggar boy and threatened to cut his throat, didn't you?"

"How do you know that?" he asked.

"I know a lot about you, Taverner," I said. "I know the way you've been working with Moll Frith. And I know that if I tell my father he'll have you swinging from the gallows faster than Moll can steal a silver cup."

"I never stole a thing," he whined.

"You helped a thief sell her stolen goods back to the

owners. I'm sure my father can find a law against that. But I'm not going to tell my father unless he threatens to hang my friend Meg for your crime," I explained.

The wild-boar eyes flickered while Michael Taverner thought about this. "I'm not admitting anything to him."

"You don't have to," I said. "I'll get Moll Frith to confess."

"Hah!" he sneered. "That woman's as tough as boiled leather. You'll never get her to admit anything even if you put her on a torture rack."

"That's a risk I'll have to take. Now I want you to walk back to Widow Atkinson's cottage. I'm going to fasten you in her turf hut till I've finished with Moll Frith. I'll set you free as soon as Meg is safe."

He scowled at me, then looked at the point of my sword. He turned and trudged back up the path. It only took a minute for me to block the door, then I was hurrying back down the path to the bridge. I'd barely reached it when I felt the ground begin to shake with drumming hooves.

Moll Frith came into sight. She was an untidy rider, rolling in the saddle with elbows spread wide. The chestnut horse slithered to a stop as she pulled on the reins. It was still moving when she jumped to the ground, her hand on the dagger at her belt. "Draw the dagger and I'll slit your throat," I said.

She was grinning, but it was a wild and desperate grin. "Young Will, my little friend. You wouldn't hurt pretty little Moll Frith, would you?"

"You won't be so pretty when you're hanging from the gallows," I told her.

Her hand moved to her throat. "You wouldn't want to see me hang."

"No," I agreed, "I wouldn't. But if I have to choose between you and Meg then I choose you."

"Ah, you've got a point there," she sighed. "I never meant for the lass to get the blame. But your father's a hard man."

"He's a stupid man," I said. "He couldn't see your game."

Moll reached inside her jerkin and pulled out her pipe. She sucked on it without lighting it. "And I don't know how you saw it, Will."

"I had a spy in the Black Bull," I said.

"Michael? Wat Grey? No! They were too well paid to let me down."

"It was a beggar boy," I said.

She looked disappointed. "And to think, I gave the young rogue a groat 'cos I felt sorry for him. That's gratitude!"

"But my father won't believe a beggar. He'll have to hear it from your own lips, Moll. You have to tell him you stole his cup."

"Or what?" she asked. Her face was open and honest as a week-old calf's.

"Or I'll tell him you have just been to Marsden Hall

and taken all the silver from the cupboard."

She looked at me in amazement. "Now, how could you know that?"

"My beggar friend heard you plan it."

"But you can't prove I took it," she said.

"But I can, Moll. How will you explain that the prints of your boots are all over the passage leading to the cupboard?"

"Are they?"

"They are. I scattered flour on the floor before I left the house and locked it. Look at your boots now," I said.

She looked down. The toes and the sides of the boots were dusted white. To my surprise she grinned. "You got me there, young Will! I didn't think you were that clever!"

"Maybe I'm not. It was my mother's idea."

"Ah! Lady Marion! Yes, it would be. I knew I never fooled her." Moll slapped her hands together and rubbed them. "Well, young Will. What are you going to do?"

"I have a plan," I told her. "First you take all the silver in your saddle bags back to Marsden Manor. Then I tell you how we get Meg free and save you from the rope you deserve."

"Your mother's plan, I suppose?"

"No," I said. Pride is a deadly sin. Master Benton tells me, but at that moment I suffered from it. "No. This plan is all my own."

CHAPTER SEVENTEEN

"And here pronounce free pardon to them all"

The silver was safely back in the cupboard and Moll was in the kitchen of Marsden Hall. I knew it was a risk handing her the pistol. It was charged with powder, so it would go off if she needed to make a frightening noise. But there was no bullet in the barrel and no one would be hurt. More important, she couldn't turn it on me.

"You'd make a wonderful footpad, Will," she said. "You're so calm. If you ever get down to London, find me and I'll buy everything you can steal. And I'll even keep open my offer to marry you!"

"I'll be going to London one day, but I hope I can live without thieving," I told her.

She shook her head sadly. "I suppose honesty's all very well for some folk. So long as you don't turn out like your father."

"Let's go and deal with him now," I said.

I took my roan mare from the stable and saddled her so I could move quickly round the estate. First I released the grumbling taverner from Widow Atkinson's turf hut. By then it was half-past twelve and the football game had only half an hour to go. Moll and I trotted to the crossroads. We didn't pass any players, so the ball must still be on Birtley land. We rode west and came across a group of Marsden men lying on the bank at the side of the road. Some were nursing wounds and all looked miserable and defeated.

"How would you like to win this football game for Marsden, you lads?" Moll cried.

They looked up at her curiously. One of the men who worked for the Marsden miller stood up stiffly. He had muscles in his shoulders that stretched his leather jerkin almost to splitting. I struggled to lift a sack of flour. This man carried one on each shoulder as if they were filled with air. "We'd love it. We have to meet those Birtley men every week at Chester-le-Street market. When we lose the football we have to suffer their smug faces and their jibes every week for the next year. I'd give anything to win – but they've got the ball and a ring of fighters round it. We just can't get through."

"Well, I've got a plan. You help me and I'll make sure you win the football game."

The men nodded, and Moll climbed down and began to explain. The men listened wide-eyed at first, then they began to smile, and then they moved quickly and eagerly back to the crossroads. Each took a handkerchief and wrapped it round his face, with a cap pulled tight down over his forehead. Moll did the same and rode off in the direction of Birtley.

Ten minutes later she trotted back, carrying the ball in one hand. "I've got it, Master Will!" she cried through the handkerchief mask as she rode on to the crossroads.

"Let the great plot go ahead!" I shouted after her.

"Yes! Let the great plot go ahead!" she laughed.

I don't think she knew she was using Mary Queen of Scots' famous words, but she enjoyed the sound of them anyway.

Crowds of men and women started to stream down the road after her. "He's got the ball!" a young apprentice cried as he ran past me.

"That's part of the game," I said.

"The masked man threatened us with a pistol! That's cheating, that it. Pistols isn't allowed!"

"The players can't use weapons," I agreed. "But that footpad isn't a player."

"I still say it's cheating!" cried the apprentice and ran on.

Soon the crossroads were packed with players and their supporters. Fighting was still going on, but most people were looking at the masked figure who sat at the entrance to the road to Marsden Village. Moll held the ball in one hand and a pistol in the other. No one dared come close to her.

Finally my father and mother came from Birtley Hall with the Birtley family and Meg. Father stood at the base of the cross while Mother, Meg and the Birtleys joined me at a safe viewpoint a little distance away on the Durham road. "What's going on here?" cried Father.

"That footpad's cheating!" Birtley players howled.

My father took a pocket watch from inside his cloak and looked at it. "There is about half a minute of this football game remaining. If the ball stays in the footpad's hand then I have to say it is on the Marsden side of the border and Marsden Manor is the winner!"

"No!" roared the Birtley mob.

"Yes!" screamed the Marsden followers.

Over the noise Father called, "I will count down from ten, then the game will be over!"

"Nine!" the crowd cried, taking up the chant. "Eight … seven … six …"

Then Moll dropped the ball.

It fell to the ground on the Marsden side of the cross-roads. The Birtley players swarmed forward and the Marsden men rushed in to block them. There was a solid mass of sprawling, brawling bodies seething like wasps round a broken nest.

Lord Birtley drew his pistol and fired in the air. "Time!" he called.

A huge groan went up from the Birtley men and many of them sank to the cold ground. A Marsden man held up the ball, just on the Marsden side of the cross. "Well done, Sir James," Lord Birtley cried. He took a few strides forward. "Where is he?"

"Who?"

"Sir James Marsden?"

Everyone turned to the cross, to where they'd last seen my father standing. "He's gone!"

"Kidnapped by masked men!" a woman cried. "While everyone was fighting for the ball, a gang of five or six men with masks snatched him and dragged him off."

"Which direction?" Lord Birtley asked.

"To Marsden!" someone told him.

"And where's the footpad?"

"Went after them!"

Lord Birtley looked stern and marched down the path to Marsden with hundreds of interested spectators in his wake. I followed on my horse. I could see over the heads of the crowd. On the village green was an interesting scene. The wooden stocks had been closed over the feet of a man with torn and stained clothing. It was my father.

Standing by his head was the masked figure of the footpad with a pistol held to his head. "Stand back, or I'll fill his brains with shot!" the footpad cried.

The crowd stopped and suddenly went silent. Lord Birtley stepped forward. "This is kidnap. You could hang for this."

"This is justice," Moll replied from behind her mask. "And you have to catch me first."

"What do you want?"

"I want to confess," Moll cried. "Sir James Marsden here has accused a girl called Meg Lumley of a theft of a silver cup." She pressed the barrel of the pistol into his neck, just under his ear. "Isn't that so, Sir James?"

"Yes," my father croaked.

"Then I wish to state, in front of all of these witnesses, that Meg Lumley is innocent. I, Francis the Footpad, took the cup." She poked him with the pistol again. "Do you believe me?"

"Yes."

"And do you pardon Meg Lumley?"

"Yes!"

Moll looked at Lord Birtley. "You heard that, Lord Birtley? You will make sure Meg Lumley does not suffer for this crime she didn't commit."

"I will," said Lord Birtley.

"I also want to say that the cup has been returned to Sir James here. Everything else that I've taken in the past month has been returned to its owner – at a small charge, of course. I am now leaving this district and I will not return. But if you send anyone after me I will shoot them. Do you understand?"

"We can't let a thief go," said Lord Birtley.

"Careful, Lord Birtley, or my finger may jump on the trigger and spread Sir James's brains over the grass," Moll threatened.

The crowd gasped. Then they laughed when someone called out, "There wouldn't be much to clear up 'cos he hasn't got many brains!" I thought I saw the man who shouted and I'm sure it was Wat Grey.

"I want an hour's start," the footpad cried. "I have a hostage. A beautiful and clever woman called Moll Frith. I am taking her with me. If I see anyone follow us, I will cut Moll Frith's throat."

Lord Birtley nodded, defeated, and looked at his watch. "You can have your hour's start, Master Footpad."

"Then, farewell!" Moll cried. She collected her horse's reins and swung herself on to its back in a single movement. She pulled back hard on the horse's bit and it reared up, pawing at the air and coming close to knocking my father's head from his shoulders. "Goodbye!" she cried happily. I was sure she was looking across at me when she said it. The crowd cheered as she turned and galloped towards Bournmoor Woods, legs and elbows flailing untidily.

The Birtley people began to wander back home and the Marsden Manor people headed for the Black Bull Tavern to celebrate their great victory. No one seemed too bothered by my father's suffering.

I jumped from my horse and ran across to him. Meg and my mother were there already He was shivering even though the sun was warm on his back. "Get me out of here."

"There is a lock, Father, and I haven't got the key."

"Then get the village carpenter with a saw so he can cut through the stocks."

"But then we'll have nowhere to punish people," I reminded him.

"Never mind that!" he said. "Just get the carpenter!"

I winked at Meg as I wandered off to the Black Bull to find the carpenter. She looked at me with a glow in her eyes. At the same time she was puzzled. She ran across the grass to join me. "How did you do it, Will?" she asked.

"Me? Are you saying I arranged the kidnap of my own father?"

"Yes."

"Why would I do a thing like that?"

"For me, perhaps?" she said.

"Perhaps."

The crowds were jammed into the doorway of the Black Bull and spilling out into the street. Meg was thin enough to burrow through and into the main room. By the time I reached her Michael the Taverner had spotted her. "Help me, Meg, for pity's sake! Serve some of these people!"

"It'll cost you sixpence," she said.

"Threepence."

"Six."

"Four."

"Six."

"Oh, very well!" Michael agreed. Meg put an apron over her new dress and started passing drinks and taking money at an amazing speed.

I finally found the carpenter crushed into a corner. He was a small, shrivelled man with over-large horny hands clasping a mug of ale. "Whan can I do for you, young Master Will?"

"My father's trapped in the stocks. He needs a carpenter to free him."

"A carpenter would be the best person," the man agreed. "But where will you find a carpenter on a Shrove Tuesday holiday?"

"You're a carpenter."

"I'm on holiday. I can do him tomorrow."

"I think he may die of the cold overnight," I said.

"In that case he won't be in a hurry for me to release him tomorrow," the man said, his pale eyes opening wide.

"I think he may pay you well," I said.

The carpenter supped his ale noisily. "I'll have to finish my beer."

"Of course."

"And go to my workshop to get some tools."

"I guessed that."

The man nodded. "Tell him he'll be free in a couple of hours at the most."

"He won't like that."

"He hasn't any choice!"

I winced at the thought of my father's anger when I passed on the message. I turned to battle my way through the crowd. I heard the carpenter's voice behind me saying, "It may just make Magistrate Marsden think twice before he sentences some other poor soul to the stocks."

The carpenter's friends laughed. I did not laugh – but I had to fight hard to smother my smile.

When I reached the village green my mother had been to Marsden Hall and returned with a warm cloak to throw over Father's shoulders. He flew into a rage when

I gave him the news about the carpenter. "Can't you go after the footpad at least?" he roared, spittle flying from his lips.

"You heard what he said? He said he'd hurt your friend Moll Frith. Do you want to risk that?"

"No-o!" he groaned.

"At least you've done what you said and driven the greatest criminal in the county away," I reminded him.

"I suppose so."

"And we did win the football match," my mother added. "So, all in all, it's been a good day." She turned to me. "We should be getting back to the hall, Will, before we get too cold."

I agreed. We looked across the village green towards the high walls that sheltered our house. There were no walls to shelter the victims who sat in the stocks and a cool breeze was blowing off the river. "What about me?" Father cried.

"We'll have a warming pan in your bed and some mulled wine for you as soon as you're free," Mother promised. We went home and left the shabby, shivering wreck in the stocks.

I don't think the stocks had ever held such a miserable villain till that day.

CHAPTER EIGHTEEN

"This my death may never be forgot"

I enjoyed playing chess against Great-Uncle George. He played like the charging knight he always thought he was. He attacked whatever the cost, and gloried in the defeats I usually gave him. "It's not the glory of winning," he said that night, "it's the thrill of the battle."

"You lost," I said.

"But I enjoyed myself," he grinned.

The fire roared and the family gathered closer round it. My father had gone straight to bed without dinner, vowing revenge and swearing that he'd never survive the marrow-chilling experience of being locked in his own stocks for two hours.

My mother was teaching Meg some new tapestry stitching.

"You said that Sir Amyas Paulet arrested Mary Queen of Scots, Lady Marsden."

"He did."

"So, how did you come to see her executed?"

My mother rubbed the girl's hair. "It was all part of Sir Francis Walsingham's game. I was just a pawn in the game like that one on Uncle George's chessboard," she sighed. She told us how her story ended ...

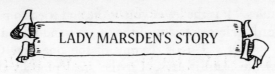

Queen Mary was arrested and led off to Tixall, and I rode back to Chartley with Sir Amyas and Morag. Sir Francis Walsingham was waiting there, looking more like a skeleton in velvet robes than ever.

The men took me to Sir Amyas's room and gave me ale to refresh me after the dusty ride. It was best ale, but it tasted sour in my mouth. After all this time I can still taste it.

"What will happen to her?" I asked. "Will she be executed?"

"Not without a trial," Sir Francis said.

"What's the charge?"

"She supported a plot to murder our rightful queen, Elizabeth," he told me.

"You have no proof."

"We have her own letter," he said.

I stayed silent. Sir Amyas said, "Perhaps young Marion thinks Babington received this letter." He pulled a packet from a drawer in his desk and handed it to me. "You may recognize it," he said.

I opened it and read it. The last lines read:

The great plot must not go ahead.
This is the order of your true Queen

MARIE R

"This was the letter Queen Mary wrote and I passed it to Gifford," I said.

Sir Amyas looked at Sir Francis and both men gave

grim smiles. "It is the letter you wrote and tried to pass on to Gifford." He reached into the drawer and pulled out a second packet. "*This* is a copy of the one that Queen Mary wrote. And it says, 'Let the great plot go ahead.' Those are the words that will put Queen Mary's head on the block, and this is the letter that you really gave to friend Gifford."

"I put my letter in the needlework basket when I'd finished it," I remembered. "I gave the Queen's letter to Morag. Someone must have switched them during the night."

"Someone did," Sir Francis agreed with a bow of his skull-like head.

"Who?" I asked. "Sir Amyas?"

The men looked at one another again. Their faces seemed expressionless, but some secret message passed between them. Sir Amyas turned back to me and watched my face carefully, then he said, "Morag changed the letters."

I gasped. "Because she wanted the Babington plot to go ahead!" I cried. "She didn't know that you were reading all the letters."

"She knew," Sir Francis said simply.

"Then she was sentencing Queen Mary to death! She'd never do that! She loves her!"

"She hates her."

"What?"

"Morag MacNeil is the niece of Lord Darnley. His family have waited nearly twenty years for revenge. When they asked me what they could do to destory the Queen, I told them to send me a girl who could spy on her from inside the household. They sent Morag and she set out to destroy her," the Secretary of State explained. "Morag is a devout Protestant and has been taught to hate the woman who murdered her uncle like a hound hates a deer. A perfect spy."

"I thought I was your spy," I said.

"You were," he said. "But we needed Morag's hatred and your brains. The Scottish girl could never have done all the writing and the coding. You were a spy – and she was set to spy on you. Just to make sure you did what we wanted." He placed a bony hand over my letter. "And it's as well that we did. The Queen's letter – the real letter – showed the poison in her heart."

"What will happen now?" I asked.

"You'll be taken to the Tower," he said.

"The west tower?" I asked. It was the place where the Queen had her apartments.

"No, child, the Tower of London!" he snapped.

I left Chartley the next day and rode south with an armed guard. I was given a small room in the Tower of London with the ghosts of all the people who'd been executed there.

After a month I was visited by Paulet and Walsingham again.

"Babington has been tortured and confessed," the Secretary of State said. "You have seen the torture implements in the Tower so that will not surprise you."

It didn't surprise me, but it sickened me. I hoped they would show Morag that chamber one day, because that was what she had sentenced Anthony Babington to. I hoped she was proud of that.

"And Queen Mary?" I asked.

Paulet's face twisted in disgust. "Mary is not a queen. She is a dead woman."

Walsingham explained more patiently that she would be taken to Fotheringhay Castle, tried and found guilty.

"How can she be guilty before her trial?" I asked.

He sniffed. "There can't be any other verdict. The two queens can't both stay alive. One of them has to die." He was right, of course.

They gave me a piece of paper to sign to say that the letter to Babington was a true copy of the one that my lady had written. Babington had destroyed the original letter and they needed me as a witness to the treason. I signed it. That was my last act of treachery against the poor lady.

In October she was put on trial. A month later she was sentenced to death. That's when Walsingham visited me in my prison. "You will be free to go when Queen Mary is dead," he said.

"There is only one place I want to go," I said.

"Tell me and I'll do what I can for you. You have served Queen Elizabeth well."

"I want to go back to my lady. I want to be with Queen Mary."

He looked at me carefully. His sharp mind was working quickly behind those hollow eyes. "Yes. A good Catholic girl would want to do that. No one knows you were part of my plot. There are a lot of Catholic gentlemen in this country who would murder you if they ever found out. Morag has gone back to the safety of her Protestant family in Scotland. You can't do that, can you? It will be good if you are seen returning to Queen Mary before she dies."

"That's not why I want to be with her," I said.

"No," he replied, "I know. You want to punish yourself. You want to watch her die. Go ahead. You can leave tomorrow for Fotheringhay."

I thought I'd reach her just in time. But Elizabeth refused to sign the execution warrant. I had three months with my lady. Walsingham and Paulet had brought her to the point of death, but they couldn't put out the fire of her spirit. "I'll die a Catholic, Marion," she told me proudly.

Winter was harsh in Fotheringhay and the cold made the Queen's twisted hands more painful than ever. Still she wrote letters every day and sewed whenever she could.

"Not everyone has the chance to die for their faith," she said cheerfully.

I wept.

But Queen Mary didn't weep when the news was finally brought to her by the Earl of Shrewsbury that bitter cold

Tuesday evening in February. When he told her she would die the next morning, she thanked him for the welcome news. "All my life I have had only sorrow," she said.

The last words she said to me as she climbed on to the scaffold were, "Queen Mary Stuart's troubles are now at an end."

My mother finished her story. I'd been listening too carefully to pay attention to the chess game and Great-Uncle George swept up one of my pieces in his huge hand. "I've captured your queen!" he chuckled.

"Yes," my mother sighed, "and once a queen is captured it's the end of the game for someone. When Mary Queen of Scots was captured it was the end for the Catholics."

"But you were free," I reminded her.

She shook her head. "All those nineteen years the Queen had been dreaming of freedom. But freedom is nothing when you've nowhere to go."

"You could have gone home," I said.

"I was too ashamed. I'd spied for Walsingham and betrayed the Catholics in England," said my mother.

"You tried your best, madam," Meg urged. "That Morag was the real traitor. You couldn't have known she'd let you down like that."

The fire lit my mother's face. "I didn't think that when I was sixteen years old. I was filled with guilt. And the horror of the execution wouldn't leave me. I once saw my brother fall from his horse and crack his head against the root of a tree. He wandered round for days not knowing who or where he was. That's how I was for such a long time."

"So where did you go?" Meg demanded.

Mother smiled at her and stroked her hair. "Sir Francis Walsingham came to visit me in Fotheringhay Castle. He said I was wise not to return home, but he would reward me. There was a rich young Protestant landowner who had done Queen Elizabeth good service. He said he'd arrange a marriage to this man who had fine estates in the north of England. I agreed because it was the only way out of that dreadful place of death."

"This man," I said. "It was Father, wasn't it?"

She nodded. "It was."

"And my son's been a good husband to you," Grandmother said sharply. "You were lucky to get a man like him."

Meg looked across at me. I said nothing. Let Grandmother keep her dreams. My mother managed a smile. "Yes. I was very lucky. He knew what I had done and still he agreed to marry me." She stood up. "I'd better go and see how the good husband is. He had a harsh lesson today."

"Life's full of harsh lessons," Grandmother said.

Next morning the frost on the lawns of Marsden Hall melted quickly in the mild air.

Father grumbled, but managed to take breakfast and

lead the family across to the church for the Ash Wednesday service. I walked alongside Meg. She was wearing her new green dress proudly.

The priest rubbed ashes into our hair to remind us that our bodies are nothing but dust and ash. Some of the villagers gasped a little as Master Benton slapped his hands firmly on their aching heads – the ones that weren't broken by the football game were aching from the effects of the Black Bull ale.

On the way back to Marsden Hall Meg pointed out snowdrops in the hedgerows. "Winter's nearly over," she said. "It's been a long and bitter one, but everything passes."

"Everything passes," my mother agreed. "Even my guilt about spying on Queen Mary. I feel better now I've finally told someone the story." She stopped. "There were snowdrops on the banks of the river outside Fotheringhay on that February Wednesday when she died," she said. She bent and picked a small bunch, then walked on with Meg on her right and me on her left. "But her body lay in Fotheringhay for weeks after the execution and the snowdrops were replaced by thistles. I saw them myself."

"The Scots have the thistle as their national flower," I explained to Meg.

She raised an eyebrow and looked at me coldly. "So much knowledge inside that head I'm surprised it doesn't burst."

I turned my face away and pretended to look at the distant coast so she wouldn't see the redness I could feel rising in my face.

My mother went on, "People said the thistles sprang from Mary Queen of Scots' tears."

"But that's not true, is it?" Meg asked.

My mother gave her the snowdrops and breathed the mild free Durham air. "It's just a story, Meg. Just a story, but with some truth in it – for the thistles were real enough. Like the fire that lit the sky for two nights after she was sentenced to death."

"A real fire?" I asked.

"It was a blazing star. Bright enough for us to read by in our prison at Fotheringhay. Some said it was the sign that the Queen was going to die."

"Do you believe in magic?" Meg asked.

"Yes, when it's the right sort of magic. And that was right for Mary Queen of Scots. Fire in the sky and tears on the ground," my mother said. "Fire and tears. She was a lady of fire and tears."

Meg clutched the snowdrops and smiled at me. "Let's go home."

The Historical Characters

The Marsden family are fictional, but the main events of Mary Queen of Scots' story are true and several of the characters were real people:

MARY QUEEN OF SCOTS 1542 – 1587 Became Queen of Scotland when she was six days old. She became mixed up in a series of scandals, including the murder of her second husband by the man who became her third husband. The disgusted Scots arrested her and forced her to give up the throne to her baby son.

Queen Mary managed to escape from her fortress prison on an island. She fled to England where her cousin, Queen Elizabeth I, promised to protect her, but locked her away in a series of castles. Queen Mary never stopped plotting to gain her freedom. She suffered considerable ill health in her life as a prisoner. Most people believe that she lived badly, but died bravely.

MARY "MOLL" FRITH 1584 – 1659 Also known as Moll Cutpurse. A London shoemaker's daughter with some education, but a wild nature. She dressed as a man, smoked a pipe and joined London street gangs. For a while she travelled the country with a theatre company. There's nothing to say she ever went to the north east where this story is set – but there's nothing to say that she didn't. She learned that selling stolen goods was badly paid. It was better to return things to their owners and get a reward. She set up a shop to return stolen property and made a fortune. Moll still did her own highway robbery from time to time and was dangerous with her sword and pistols.

SIR FRANCIS WALSINGHAM C.1530 – 1590 Elizabeth made Walsingham her Secretary of State and he created a network of spies. He discovered Catholic priests in hiding, such as Campion at Lyford Grange. They were tortured for information and executed with horrible cruelty. Thanks to Walsingham's work Elizabeth survived every plot against her. His greatest triumph was uncovering the Babington plot. A clever and ruthless man.

ANTHONY BABINGTON 1561 – 1586 When Mary Queen of Scots was a prisoner in Sheffield, young Anthony served for a short while as her page. From then on he dreamed of setting her free. Queen Mary put him in touch with another plot that was being hatched at the same time – a plot to assassinate Elizabeth. Sir Francis Walsingham knew all about both plots, but let them go ahead until he could prove Queen Mary was part of the treason. Queen Mary's coded letter to Babington led to his being tortured to confess, then to his death by hanging, drawing and quartering.

GILBERT GIFFORD Came from an old Catholic family, but failed in his attempt to become a priest. Gifford seems to have enjoyed spying. He went to France and learned all the plots to free Queen Mary. But when he returned to England he was caught and taken to Walsingham. He not only betrayed the plots, but offered to change sides and work for Elizabeth I. His scheme to send letters in beer barrels led to the deaths of Queen Mary, Babington and many other plotters. He left England again before the trial and before Catholics could take their revenge on him.

SIR AMYAS PAULET C.1536 – 1588 Mary Queen of Scots' last jailer and her harshest. He was a fierce hater of Catholics and was determined to see Queen Mary die. Strangely, Queen Elizabeth told Paulet he could "find some way to shorten the life" of Queen Mary – that is, murder her – yet he refused. He wanted justice and a proper execution.

The Time Trail

1533 Elizabeth Tudor is born, the second daughter of King Henry VIII.

1534 Henry VIII quarrels with the Catholic Church and makes himself head of the Protestant Church of England.

1542 Mary Stuart is born in Scotland and her father, James V, dies a week later. Baby Mary is Queen of Scots. She is also the niece of Henry VIII, so she has a claim to the English throne if Henry's three children die.

1547 Henry VIII dies and his son Edward takes the throne. He's a sickly boy.

1553 Edward dies and his sister, Mary, comes to the throne. She is a Catholic and tries to turn England back into a Catholic state. Hundreds of Protestants are burned. A year later she marries her Spanish cousin, Philip of Spain.

1558 Mary dies and Henry's last child, his daughter Elizabeth, comes to the throne. England becomes a Protestant country again, but Elizabeth is always worried that the Catholics will kill her and put Mary Queen of Scots on the English throne.

1565 Mary Queen of Scots marries her cousin, Henry Stuart, Lord Darnley. This is not popular in Scotland and Queen Mary has to crush a rebellion.

1566 Queen Mary's favourite secretary, David Riccio, is murdered in her room. Her husband Lord Darnley is behind the plot and she never forgives him.

1567 Lord Darnley is murdered and Queen Mary is suspected and arrested. She gives up the Scottish throne to her one-year-old son, James VI.

1568 Queen Mary escapes to England where her cousin, Elizabeth I, protects her. But Mary is a threat to Elizabeth's throne – Catholics could rise up in support of her – so Elizabeth protects herself by locking Mary away.

1584 London. Mary Frith is born. She will grow up to become a famous pickpocket, highway robber and dealer in stolen goods.

1586 Catholic Anthony Babington plots to free Queen Mary and assassinate Elizabeth. This is one of many such plots, but this time Mary Queen of Scots writes to say she supports it. Her letter is read by Elizabeth I's spies. Queen Mary is brought to trial and found guilty.

1587 Elizabeth finally signs the execution warrant and Mary Queen of Scots is beheaded at Fotheringhay Castle. Crafty James VI of Scotland, Queen Mary's son, stays friendly with Elizabeth.

1588 The Catholic invasion from Spain finally arrives when the Armada sails to England. It is defeated. Even if it had succeeded, it arrived too late to rescue Mary Queen of Scots.

1603 Elizabeth dies and James VI of Scotland becomes King of England. The Stuart family of Scotland have replaced the Tudor family in England.

1659 Moll Frith dies at the age of 75.

You will also enjoy

The Prince of Rags and Patches

A visitor comes to Marsden Manor, bearing letters from the dying Queen Elizabeth to James VI of Scotland.

A man lies in Bournmoor Woods – murdered.

And Will Marsden, aided and abetted by Meg the serving girl, sets out to find the killer.

Meanwhile, Will is puzzling over the story of his Marsden ancestor who followed Richard III into battle, was mixed up in the mysterious deaths of the Princes in the Tower ... and whose meeting with a prince of rags and patches gives Will the clue he needs to solve the murder mystery.

'Nemo · me · impune'

Tudor Terror

The King in Blood Red and Gold

When handsome, foppish Hugh Richmond turns up at Marsden Manor, claiming to be one of Queen Elizabeth's spies asking for help, Will and his grandfather seize on the chance for adventure!

Riding north to Scotland, Grandfather tells Will how his own father fought at the Battle of Flodden Field in the service of Henry VIII. Then as now, there were desperate skirmishes on the Borders between the English and the Scots Reivers – cattle thieves.

Neither of them realizes quite what danger Hugh is leading them into ... and it seems that all their quick wit and courage will not get them out.

Luckily, Meg is very clever ...

The Knight of Stars and Storms

The Marsden family are in desperate trouble. If they can't pay their debts, they will lose their home. So Will and his father, Sir James – and Meg who refuses to be left behind – set sail for London with a cargo of coal to sell, to save the family fortunes.

But someone is out to get them ... and when Sir James recounts his adventures sailing the Pacific with Sir Francis Drake twenty-five years ago, Will and Meg are able to work out a plan of action.

The Lord of the Dreaming Globe

A man with one eye is trying to kill young Will Marsden.

All Will wants is to get to Stratford where Master William Shakespeare has promised him work, but somebody seems to think he has important information.

And when Master Shakespeare's daughter Judith is kidnapped, Will and Meg discover that the world of theatre is not what it seems. Certain actors are spying on their countrymen, on the orders of the Queen herself …

It takes Will's courage, Meg's ingenuity, and the genius of Shakespeare himself to get out of the desperate plot they find themselves mixed up in.

The Queen of the Dying Light

Will Marsden gets to meet Queen Elizabeth herself in a thrilling adventure that involves the famous magician Doctor Dee, a witch hunt, and a wild ride from London to Scotland.

to be published in 1999